He Doesn't Follow the Script

Lotte Søs Farran-Lee

BALBOA.PRESS

A DIVISION OF HAY HOUSE

Balboa Press books may be ordered through booksellers or by contacting:

Balboa Press
A Division of Hay House
1663 Liberty Drive
Bloomington, IN 47403
www.balboapress.com
1 (877) 407-4847

Because of the dynamic nature of the Internet, any web addresses or links contained in this book may have changed since publication and may no longer be valid. The views expressed in this work are solely those of the author and do not necessarily reflect the views of the publisher, and the publisher hereby disclaims any responsibility for them.

The author of this book does not dispense medical advice or prescribe the use of any technique as a form of treatment for physical, emotional, or medical problems without the advice of a physician, either directly or indirectly. The intent of the author is only to offer information of a general nature to help you in your quest for emotional and spiritual well-being. In the event you use any of the information in this book for yourself, which is your constitutional right, the author and the publisher assume no responsibility for your actions.

Any people depicted in stock imagery provided by Getty Images are models, and such images are being used for illustrative purposes only.
Certain stock imagery © Getty Images.

Print information available on the last page.

ISBN: 978-1-9822-4028-8 (sc)
ISBN: 978-1-9822-4030-1 (hc)
ISBN: 978-1-9822-4029-5 (e)

Library of Congress Control Number: 2019920853

Balboa Press rev. date: 01/06/2020

Contents

Chapter 1   The Script...1

Chapter 2   Heading Home from Interrail............................3

Chapter 3   New Steps in Life.. 13

Chapter 4   The Pain of Not Seeing....................................19

Chapter 5   When the Pain Doesn't Leave 29

Chapter 6   New York.. 41

Chapter 7   Granddad 53

Chapter 8   Moving On 59

Chapter 9   The Pink Bike 65

Chapter 10 A Wedding 73

Chapter 11 Fighting the Script 85

Chapter 12 The Priest 101

Chapter 13 Shreya 109

Chapter 14 Tripping in Signs 125

Chapter 15 A Restaurant.. 139

Chapter 16 Separation...147

Chapter 17 I See You..151

Chapter 18 Rome Again..165

Chapter 19 Can You Not, Not Listen to the Script? 175

Chapter 20 A Wedding in Varenna 181

Chapter 21 183

1

The Script

"How much do you really have to say? Honestly? Lay your hand on your heart and tell me, do you really think we're in control?"

"Well, I don't know."

"I didn't ask you that. I asked if you thought we have a free will or whether it's all written."

Katrin was getting a bit pissed off with this man. She had agreed to come to this talk about the script, but she hadn't really felt the need for him to expose her to everyone.

"I did choose you for a reason. Would you like to share?"

He was really a pain in the ass, this guy. She took a deep breath. She had a choice: she could shut her mouth, she could walk away, or she could answer him. The question was just so provocative. Because she had in fact thought about it a lot; that was why she was sitting here in the first place.

She took a moment. It felt like five minutes but was only a few seconds.

"Well, then … since you are so insistent. I have actually given it a lot of thought. I believe it's both, and one can't act without the other."

"So you did have an opinion."

Katrin thought he was a bit too cocky, smiling out into the room at his triumph in getting her to talk.

She continued without reacting to his hovering. "I believe that certain events we have no power to change; those will happen no matter what, and even if you try to make a decision to avoid them, they will happen anyway. They're in the script, so to speak. But apart from that, I do think we have free will to make choices. But then again, those choices: where do they come from? Because our choices are based on our state of mind, state of feeling, and who owns this? I know it's our brains that perceive it, and they generate the outcome, but still … I'm fascinated by it, because really, do we have anything to say?"

The guy, and God forbid even with a name like Hans, looked a bit long in the face. Clearly he was surprised that she had given it so much thought, although what she had delivered was short. She couldn't help feeling a bit high that he looked taken aback.

"I like your thoughts. Why have you thought about it so much?"

"It's a long story, but to cut it short, I envision a lot that happens before it actually manifests, and no matter how hard I try to avoid certain things at times, they do manifest. So I believe that I can't change them—even if I can choose the way I react to them. But then again I ask myself where do the choices come from?"

"Thank you for your contribution."

The idiot clearly didn't want to get too involved with her thinking right here. But she had made her point.

"You got him, babe." Rikke, her longtime friend, couldn't help approving Katrin for her words. "You rock!"

"Yeah, I did." Katrin gave her a smile. She was in the process of writing her next book, *It Is Said that There Is a Script*. It was based on the thoughts and experiences she had had over the years, first with *My Italian Angel* and then *He Doesn't Follow the Script*.

It had all been a constant repetition of her discovery that a script was in action in life and her insights into how it all was connected. Then Rikke had suggested that she start writing the next book, *It Is Said that There Is a Script*, and she thought it was a great idea, so she began to do her research. Anyway, that was how she had ended up here, with Hans. But she didn't get anything out of it that she hadn't already known in some way—or so she thought.

2

Heading Home from Interrail

He just stood there, his eyes capturing the nothingness. He had forgotten what he was doing, heard the others in the background, but was not present with their words. He felt alive more than he ever had—and dead at the same time. He knew she was a very important key to his life. He had seen her in a split second, and in the next she was gone ....

That perplexity of heaven and hell was present at the same instant. He couldn't understand. Why had he not been given the chance to be in contact with her? What was she thinking? Who was she? Where did she come from? Would he ever see her again? And why this intense feeling of knowing that it was *her*, and no one else could ever not be her?

He was only eighteen; his life was still to unfold. He was in charge, he knew what he wanted, and then this deep, deep sense of an inner pain that had been undefined in his soul had just gotten a face. But what could he use that for? Nothing! It was just pure crap to meet her and have her disappear.

"What's going on, Michael? Where have you gone? You look like you're stoned."

Lars, his brother, and their two friends were repeating themselves, laughing, trying to get through to him.

"I saw her."

"What do you mean by that?"

"The woman."

"What woman?"

"The one and only."

He looked straight into his brother's eyes with a very determined look. Lars knew this look so well, like an inside-out sushi roll. When he got that look from Michael, he knew that there was nothing to do; no one in the world could make him change. It was his spiritual side, the one they all laughed at: neither Mom, Dad, their sister, or he understood what Michael did, but they also knew that he had a special connection with something they didn't know. It was one of these moments now.

Lars felt uncomfortable when Michael gave him this look. Normally he could escape it, but their friends were watching them, so he ventured to make a bit of a joke on Michael. He hated it. When Michael had this look, he was right in some way, and now again Lars was in a situation of putting Michael in the wrong. He knew Michael thought he was a fraud when he sold him out—and rightly so.

"Stop it now. There are many beautiful women out there in the world."

"You know, the one and only, the very special one. I saw her, and she saw me, and now she is gone? I just can't believe it!"

"How would you know, Michael?"

"You know that feeling in me. I just know!"

Lars gave him a long look deep into his eyes; he had no words. What could he say? He knew that Michael was right in his way, but why did he want his approval? He'd never understood him anyway, and Michael knew that.

"Come on, let's go, Michael. We have a train to catch, and you still haven't found your damn ticket. It's not the end of the world."

Lars and his friends laughed.

He gave Lars a deep, angry look. *Ahh, what the fuck, they don't know shit anyway! Where is that ticket? —Finally, here it is; then I'm not completely lost.* "It's here! I found it. Let's go."

"Woohoo, Michael, then there is still hope in the world."

They all laughed, grabbed their bags, and started walking toward track 16. Their train was about to depart for Milan. From Milan they were changing to Zürich, then Hamburg, and then finally Copenhagen.

It had been a long, fun, and now quite exhausting trip. They had been all the way down to Corfu from Copenhagen. The idea had felt great going by train all the way to Greece, but now heading home, it just felt as though it would never end. They had stayed ten days at Karda beach, camping in a bungalow. They had been so pissed, drinking a hell of a lot of B52s. Too much sun, too many beautiful women, and too much alcohol.

But fuck, it had been fun for Michael. He had kissed one woman. He believed that she had believed it was the big love; he sure was not on that road with her. He had been an idiot in the end. Hopeless holiday love affair. He always crossed the line and looked as if he was attached, when it was just meant to be a fling.

The other three were walking ahead of him. He glanced back and looked around, hoping to see her again. Hoping that a miracle would drop down in his hands. What would he do if he saw her? Would he run? Would he wave? All just guesses; he had no idea.

They started running now. The train was leaving in three minutes, and it was not in fashion to stay one more day in Rome. They wanted to leave.

All thoughts left the brain. The legs took over, and they moved fast. They jumped on the train seconds before the doors closed.

He stood for a while catching his breath, seeing the platform moving slowly away from him, Rome slipping through his fingers … slipping *her* through his fingers too. He closed his eyes and centered himself. He had to let her go. Maybe she would come back. He followed the others to his seat, sank into it, and closed his eyes, his senses closing down awareness of the world around him.

It had been such an incredible second; she had seen *him*, he knew, and she knew that he knew that this was it. But then, just as the moment had felt like a lifetime, it had vanished. He disappeared behind the three guys standing with her from the train, where one of them had touched her lips with his last night.

She felt the warmth and depth of his eyes burned into hers like a soul print melting her. She almost wanted to scream to the three guys to move their ass, but the noise and the craziness of Roma Termini were just too loud. It was as if she was inside a bell, and all reality had left the scene. When the three guys finally moved, he was gone.

She just looked at the spot where she'd glimpsed him, only to see a special spot of light from the sun just touching where he'd stood. He had left the scene, but the light was still on.

"Hellooo, Katrin, are you here? I'm actually … We are actually trying to get in touch with you!"

"Sorry, I got lost in my own world. What's up?"

"Yeah, you can say that. Do you want to go to Corfu with them?"

Her friend nodded at the three guys, all of them staring at her, to get a response. She was lost in that moment with his eyes, with that magnetic moment she had shared with a stranger, even though he didn't feel like a stranger.

"Yes, sorry, I think it's a perfect idea. Let's go."

The three guys grabbed their bags, happy with the decisions that had been made, and started walking ahead when her friend looked her straight in her eyes, with a *What happened?* look. Her eyes replied, *I'll tell you later.* She smiled to her friend, tired, confused, happy, and sad … that look.

Her mind drifted. It was not that he was just sexy and beautiful; He was everything, and now without any words, any touch, any connection, no name, no sound, he was gone—as if God had placed him there with a special dust, only to take that dust away again, and yet in some way she felt the dust would never disappear from her again.

As they headed toward their train, she was still looking around to see if luck would bring him back.

"What track are we leaving from?" she shouted to the guys.

"Track fifteen," Kristian said.

"That's brilliant. I see track sixteen now."

"Wow, you are just super sharp."

They all laughed.

"Yes, I know."

She laughed back. God, she was tired and confused and now going to Corfu with three guys, one from Copenhagen that she had already kissed last night. What a mess. The guy Thomas turned his head to smile at her, hoping for more.

What a mess. I'm not even sure I want to go to Corfu, but it's like the only thing I can do now. I have no other suggestions, and in a way I just want to go home, more than anything. Maybe that was all I needed to come for. To meet his eyes. And then Thomas—I mean, what to do really? Let it go, Katrin, let it go.

They approached track 15, and as they entered the platform, the train on track 16 was closing its doors. The whistle of the conductor made sure that everyone knew it was departing. She stopped for a moment and looked at the train that was leaving, checking the sign to see where it was going: Milan. In a second she felt she would rather have been on that train than the one going to Brindisi, which then would take her to Corfu and specifically Karda beach, to camp in a bungalow that now was waiting for her and a bed where that special dust had already been sleeping a couple of days ago—but that, she could not know.

They smelled like shit. They had been going for almost three days without any shower, and it felt to embarrassing to sit next to any other passengers. They decided to stand in the hallway, sometimes sitting on their bags, most of the time half sleeping, drinking some Coca-Cola, eating shitty sandwiches.

They were tired. The high energy had gone very low, and no one was really talking to each other anymore.

It was the last stretch from Hamburg to Copenhagen, and they were heading toward the harbor and the ferry taking them to Denmark. Michael was in his own world, thinking about what he was going to do after the summer holiday. He had three weeks left at his summer job as a bartender in central Copenhagen. He was terrible at the job, but it paid well, they had fun and drank a lot after closing, and there was a lot of flirting. He couldn't really understand why he hadn't been fired, but he was grateful for having been able to stay for so long.

When the summer ended, he would start at Copenhagen Business School. He wanted to do well in business; he had plans and wanted to build his own thing, create money. He and Lars had gotten a small apartment near Nyhavn, and it was perfect, centrally located and super cool. He felt like he was on top of the world, and he had just started.

He was half sleeping, half awake, hearing the rhythm of the train along the tracks in the background. His mind fell into silence from his many thoughts, and a dust green field with morning haze appeared in his inner sight. The silence in the landscape was so deep that he was holding his breath while observing his inner picture. In the middle of the mist a woman in a white long dress was walking slowly toward him. He felt a wisdom was with her, something that was important for him. He slowly observed her graceful steps as she walked, her feet moving and arms swinging.

He had not been able to see her face, but suddenly he saw straight into *her* eyes, the woman from Roma Termini, the special one. It was her, she was coming to him in his dreams. He held his breath and looked deeply in her eyes; she smiled, and he smiled back. The silence was massive, and his heart was pounding, his mouth all dry. He wanted to ask her so many things, and yet nothing came out of his mouth. He knew that she knew his thoughts anyway. He kept looking at her, waiting for her to deliver her message. He knew that when a specific kind of pictures came into his dreams, they came with a message for him. This was one of them.

She gently touched his right cheek with her hand, and he closed his eyes to feel her fully. The feeling of her hand burned into his cells. He opened his eyes again and saw her warmness and love. He knew he loved her.

"I will come. We will meet, but live and love your journey." She smiled at him, gave him a soft kiss on his cheek, and vanished like dust into the dust green field.

The picture left his inner world, and he knew she had left.

He woke up only to see the train carriage in a mess of bags, the smell of too much human, burned rubber, and diesel, his friends dozing off. He looked at his watch; they would soon be there. He felt he had been on a long inner trip, but he knew she would enter his life again at some point. He stretched, took a sip of his water, and stared out in the carriage van. A strong message had arrived. He knew he had to live with it and let it go at the same time.

He had experienced such messages before. He had always tried to tell Lars, his sister Lisa, and his mom and dad about these pictures or small movies that came to him now and then to tell him about the future. They had never understood, and then later he had stopped telling them. Only his grandfather understood him. He was his special one. He was the one that always knew what was going on in his head. One look from his grandfather could mean the world to him, because he knew he understood. Likewise, his grandfather knew that Michael was special, that he could understand something that others couldn't. The bond was special and strong … everybody knew.

"You got to wake up, guys; we are soon there."

"Thanks, Michael."

They all stretched, yawning, and tried to get themselves together a bit. It was time to leave the train. The ferry was ready to take them back home. Everything was in a way the same, and at the same time nothing would never ever be the same again. He knew the trip had changed that—she had changed that.

"So, what was that all about? Why did you look so lost at the Termini?"

They were alone in the carriage van down to Brindisi. The three guys had gone to the food wagon, and they had it all to themselves for a bit of time. They were quite funny, although Katrin hadn't really had that much time alone with her friend. Basically almost none since they left home, and she missed it.

"Well, I was glancing around the station and at one point, one guy was standing there, good looking and all that, but it was not just that. He stared at me, and I did it back, and it was as if everything in life just stopped. It's hard to explain, but it was *him*. I'm 100 percent sure, it's *him*, the one and only, and now he is gone, thanks to our three dear friends when they were walking toward us at the Termini. I could have screamed at them, but then Thomas would have noticed and I have already been an ass once, you know."

She smiled to her friend.

"So you're saying you met the one and only at Roma Termini, and you know that just by looking in his eyes, and now he is gone?"

"Yes, that's exactly how it is."

"You're crazy, you know that, right, love?"

Her friend gave her a cheeky smile. She knew she was crazy in a good way; that made her life magical. She dared to do things that were not logical, and she trusted that source within her more than anything else in the world.

"I know it's ridiculous, but I know it's true. It's him; I just don't know anything else. What the fuck! Gotta let it go now. Life will unfold it, but it just seems so—not fair. Anyway don't tell Thomas this, right? Maybe I want to kiss him some more."

"No, no, I won't."

They laughed, lit a cigarette, took a sip of an old beer that stood on the little table, and were singing an awful song. They were happy, tired, and dirty, but life seemed to lie in the shadow of a huge wisdom, light and painful at the same time. Soon they would reach Brindisi and the ferry to Corfu. Such a stupid thing to go all the way to Greece by train. It didn't seem like a great idea, but then again, that's the way life is. Life was leading them.

"Katri-i-in, come on, darling. Hurry up. We need to leave the train now."

"Sorry, I'm coming now. Where are we?"

"Brindisi, my darling. You must have fallen into a really deep sleep. It was so hard to wake you."

"Sorry, I was way gone. Where are the guys?"

"Just over there buying tickets for us."

"How are you, Katrin? You look completely off."

"I know, I had a weird dream that I was meeting him in a dream, on a dust green field. He was standing there and looked at me, and I was walking toward him. Then I told him something, but I can't remember what, and I kissed him gently on his cheek. It felt so real, like he was just in my hands. I guess that's why I'm a bit off."

"When you say *him*, you mean the guy from Roma Termini, right?"

"Yes, it was him. It's strange. I feel something was just spot on. Like it was the first time in my life it had happened!"

"Hmmm, must say it sounds strange, but anyway—I mean I can see by your face that something has hit you really deep. Come here and get a hug."

They hugged a long time. No words, just an understanding of something special.

"Come, it's time to board the ferry."

"I know."

Katrin slipped out of her arms and took her backpack. She found a seat on the top of the deck, put her legs up on the backpack, and closed her eyes, absorbing the sun. She heard the voice of the ferry as it said goodbye to the harbor, the engines started, and the ferry pulled out. Sorrow and a deep joy together filled her heart; it was a heart that was truly shattered for the first time in her life.

Lotte Søs Farran-Lee

Up north
In Germany
On its way
To
Denmark.
A heart
A shattered too
Was
Pumping
Sorrow
Love
Joy
Because of
A
Knowing
That
A special one
Was out
There

Questions
Were
In
The air
Was it to unfold?
Was this love
A part of their
Script?

3

New Steps in Life

"Happy birthday to you, happy birthday to you. Happy birthday, dear Katrin. Happy birthday to you. Woohoo!"

Everybody was singing out loud, clapping their hands, eager to celebrate her fortieth birthday. It was almost midnight, and they had been drinking for many hours now. It was not the first time the song had been sung that night. Everyone was so happy, it was an amazing night.

She had hired a restaurant in the harbor of Copenhagen with a magnificent view over the water. The June evening was exceptional: the weather was mild without a wind, and the warmth of the sunny day had lingered late. It was one of those special Nordic summer evenings when you feel the sun will never leave. She had wanted to be celebrated with style, so she had put a huge party together.

"Thank you, my lovely ones. Cheers!" Katrin called out to all her friends and family. She was happy at heart. It had been some rough years, and she now felt she had made a mark, that she was creating a new beginning.

"Come on, Katrin, you sexy one."

Her friend Sebastian smiled at her and put an arm around her waist to pull her tight into him. He gave her a gentle kiss, while swinging his glass of wine in his other hand.

"Let's go sit on the terrace."

"Yes, let's do that my beautiful friend."

They had been friends for many years, since Interrail. They had met on their way down to Italy, she had been kissing with his friend Thomas that summer, while she had been dreaming of the man she had seen on the Roma Termini. Thomas and she had only lasted that summer, but she had remained very close friends with Sebastian since then.

He had been there in all her ups and downs, as she had been there for his.

"Think about it, Katrin, we have known each other for twenty-two years now."

"Yes, it's amazing. You are a true diamond in my life."

"Cheers to you, my darling. May you be blessed with true magic."

"Thank you. It's incredible that I'm forty now. I have always been looking forward to that, feeling my life will truly unfold now in the shape that is me. That the pain is no longer the priority in my life."

"I had never heard anyone looking forward to forty before, Katrin, but it's so you. You always do and feel everything upside down. That is why you're so refreshing."

He was smiling at her, and she smiled back. She knew, and she loved him for always embracing her differentness. He never argued back when she had to do and experience life her way.

They sat on the terrace alone, and he was smoking a cigarette. They sat in silence with her leaning into him. She was so grateful for Stine, Sebastian's wife, that she could embrace her friendship with Sebastian with a fully open heart. She was an amazing soul. She and Sebastian had four kids, lived up north of Copenhagen in a huge house, and nothing was missing: love, money, and joy. They were so special to her. They had been there all the way through her divorce from Mads. Even though it had been a very gentle one, it had been rough. It had been for the best, and they were still close friends.

Stine and her other close friend Rikke came out to the terrace with a bottle of champagne.

"You gotta have a glass of champagne, Katrin."

"You're a star, Stine. Absolutely."

Stine filled three glasses with champagne.

"Congratulations, Katrin, may the stars be with you now."

They all screamed out in the night.

"Thank you. I love you all."

"We love you too."

She took a sip from her glass and felt the cool, sparkling freshness of the champagne touching her tongue. She let it breathe in her mouth before she swallowed. She felt a deep peace within her, watching the shadows of the buildings in the harbor, the moonlight glancing lighting up the water. She felt happier than she had in years; she felt peace within.

It's only seven months since my Italian angel, dear Angelo, left me and I left him. It's only that short amount of time since I completed my deep and painful journey, and now life feels so completely different. Like I'm finally starting to be able to live. I have learned how to love; now I just hope the one I'm to be with will show up soon so I can love unconditionally again. I miss it. It's been two years since the divorce, and I just would like things to blossom again. It has been so hard on so many levels.

An Angel
Had come.
He had
Showed her
Love.
Love when
It had no
Agendas.
Only
Her
Heart had
Been asked
Over and over
To love,
Love,
Love.
And so she
Had
Done.

"Are you going to Pitigliano in the beginning of September to Kristian's wedding? Because then Sebastian and I thought we could go there together and find a house where we all could stay."

"Yes, I am. That would be brilliant, Stine. When were you thinking about leaving?"

"We thought we could fly to Rome on the Thursday and take one day in Rome. Then we could rent a car and go up north in the late afternoon to Pitigliano. Maybe you could show us some of your Rome?"

"That sounds brilliant. I would love that. I can book the flight tickets. That would be so much fun. I really hope that Kristian and Giovanna are going to have a fantastic marriage. It was so hard with Kristian and his first wife—shit, I forgot her name!"

"Malene. You are getting old now; you're forty. That's why you can't remember."

Sebastian laughed

"You never know. But I think it's so utterly fantastic crazy that he just met her, and they are getting married, and then he is going to live there in Rome."

"Yes, it's amazing," Rikke said.

"Yes it is. But come on, we have to go and dance our asses off now."

Sebastian took the lead with all the ladies. The night had become an early morning before they were heading home. A new beginning had been celebrated.

She woke up with a headache that had not been present for many years. It had been such an amazing night. They had been drinking, screaming, hugging, laughing, and dancing all night long. She had so many blessed people in her life. She was just one big smile.

Her clothes were spread out all over her floor. She had hired a hotel room in the center of Copenhagen so she could just crash after the party. Room service were on their way with her breakfast after her bath.

She drew the curtains aside and let the sun find its space in the room. She drifted to the bathroom and set the hot steamy water to fill the tub.

She sank into the water and closed her eyes, feeling the damp in the room and the hot water touching her skin, making her body warm and soft. She could feel the tiredness in her body. Her mind drifted away.

Seven months ago the airplane had taken her home from Rome, the first time in her life she felt that home was Denmark. A long journey felt complete. A long yearning in her soul felt as though it had been seen and accomplished, as if the knowing she had longed for had found peace in her soul. She still knew that a man was to arrive in her life, but she didn't know when. She had felt the longing of knowing what unconditional love felt like when that knowing entered every cell of her body and soul. It had come to an end as she left Rome.

She had many years ago been shown an inner vision, that a man would come, a man that had a higher purpose in her life. That was when she had fucked up her soul, because she wanted to learn and receive that in her life, more than anything. It had taken her out on an inner and outer journey, and she could not even believe how much it had affected her life. It had for a period of seven years been her only focus in the world to heal that part.

And now seven months later, forty years old, she felt the new beginning was hers for real, not life pulling her around in pain, but for her to create in the world.

She took a deep breath, feeling so true and honest toward herself and excited about the next new thing to show up.

Slowly she awoke again, pulled herself up from the tub, and covered herself in a thick white bathrobe. Her skin was red and warm, and she felt an inner warmth and lust. She lay down on the bed and opened the robe, letting the sun touch her naked body, and brought herself to release.

Noon
Arrived
Checked out
Legs
Moving
One
Foot at a time
Slowly
Moving.
The sun
Touching
Her.
Passing
The marble church
Went inside
Sat down.
Folded her

Hands
Asked for guidance
Steps,
Visions,
On her next
Steps
To be
Taken.
On her
Journey
To unfold
The script
That was
Already
Written.
What choices
Was hers?
And what
Was not?
What was
Already in
The script?
Her intention
Of knowing
Was deep!

4

The Pain of Not Seeing

Why did it have to happen right now? He was super busy, and he had no time to stand here with this stupid young man. He had seen a truck turning and was afraid that it would hit the guy on the bicycle, so he had gently pulled his BMW a bit back for the guy to pass and had then hit a young very hot-tempered guy's car.

"Sorry, it's all my fault, but I don't think anything happened."

"It's a brand-new car. I have just driven three thousand kilometers in it, and now you've scratched it!"

"Relax, I just backed slowly into your car. Not that much can have happened."

"Yes, it has."

"No, it just can't have been. I can see a little mark on the number plate, but that's it. I was hardly moving."

The guy was falling down now, nothing was to see, but he just couldn't let it go. He was jabbing away and Michael only registered half of his words.

What an obnoxious asshole. In a hurry he handed over his business card. *Michael*, it said, *CEO*, with a phone number and an email.

What it didn't say was that he was forty, in an unhappy relationship, stubborn as a donkey and not listening to his inner voice.

He was on his way to a meeting with his friend Kristian. He had just secured a big business deal and felt great but also empty. He had done it so many times now with huge success. He had created many businesses, and they had all done amazingly well. The breadth of the inner emptiness came present to him, but he shut it down as always. He used his special senses in business, always knowing the next move, seeing opportunities when no one else did. With everyone else, he trusted that special side of him, and Lars had long ago given up fighting that side of Michael. He knew that

Michael was always right in business when it came to this, and it was good for Lars too, as they were in business together. But when Michael took a look at himself using his deep knowing he shut off. He carried a pain that he was too frightened to see. He knew he was different, but he didn't want to admit it. He wanted to be like all the others.

What a day, it seems like I need to see something I don't see. I'm so tired of these arguments with Marianne, like the one I had with her this morning. It's like this every fucking day. It's the same, over and over. I don't get it. She knows who I am, or at least I think so; maybe she doesn't. She says it's okay to be home and take care of it all, but then she is angry with me all the time. I know I'm working all the time, but she has known that always. She wanted the children, not me. I love them, but still—what the fuck is wrong? What is it that I'm not getting and wanting to see? I'm giving her all the right things, but it's still not good enough. We don't make love; we don't laugh. Sometimes I think we should just end it. But then I would look like the one that can never adjust to the world. And now this stupid guy.

Michael started his black BMW and turned left. He was going to meet Kristian at a café near Kristian's home at Bryggen. He couldn't believe that Kristian was moving to Rome. Kristian was an architect and had just met Giovanna last winter when he had been on a conference in Rome. Suddenly she had just been there, and they knew in that second that they had to be together.

Michael smiled to himself. He was happy for Kristian. Kristian had had such a shitty marriage with Malene. They had tried too hard all the time, and in the end he had just slept with an unknown woman, desperate from the pain they were going through. That had killed it between Kristian and Malene, or maybe it had already died when children never came. Right now that seemed like a blessing.

Kristian could be such an ass toward women and had always slept around even when he had girlfriends, but now … Michael had never seen him so happily in love as when he was with Giovanna. He was sure that Kristian now had found the one he would treasure and not treat her like something that had nothing to do with him.

Michael could see a bit of himself in Kristian, the one who didn't want to settle for real, the one who didn't really love the woman he was

Lotte Søs Farran-Lee

with. But he wasn't an asshole like Kristian. He liked to do it right in some respectful manner.

Giovanna had been to Denmark once, and Marianne and Michael had been out for dinner with her and Kristian.

She was beautiful and full of confidence, and he could easily sense that Marianne wasn't at peace with that. Marianne didn't have much confidence in herself. He knew that somehow reflected on him, but at least he covered it up with good clothes, a successful business, a beautiful wife and kids, and a nice house. He knew he was not true to his heart, fearing that life wouldn't be as spectacular then. That night when looking at Kristian with Giovanna, he could not stop thinking about *her*, "my Roman girl." He had often drifted away in the conversation, thinking that he would be as happy as Kristian was with Giovanna if he could be with *her*.

He had sensed that Marianne was studying him across the table, uncertain about him, but he had tried to ignore it. He knew it would come later.

When they had left the restaurant, he had fiercely hugged Kristian. Kristian knew him well, and he knew that Roman girl was in Michael right now. He smiled at him. He had given Giovanna a hug and they had said "Ciao-ciao." He had watched them walking away, truly in love, only to then see Marianne's furious face.

He just looked at her and knew what was coming.

"Why are you all gone? Why are you so happy when you look at Kristian and Giovanna? I think you look at her too much! Is she prettier than me? Why don't you look at me like that?"

Her questions and blame went on and on, and he was just overwhelmed by the accusations. He kept silent, just looking out into the nothingness, trying to find some new words. But nothing had been given him.

"Why are you so silent? Can't you say anything? I have just asked you so many questions and you don't say anything. Don't you care? Don't you care about me and the children? Don't you care about us?"

"I'm trying, Marianne, but I just don't know what to say. We're out with one of my best friends, and you're just sitting there through the whole dinner and can't smile or be a part of any conversation, and then you come out here and blame me for everything—again."

He was silent for a moment and just looked at her. Then he continued.

"I know I'm an asshole for not being there all the time, but you have always known that. What is it now? I can't do anything right, and I'm sick and tired of this conversation. Why don't you participate when we're out? You just look like you hate being there."

"You just don't get it, do you?"

"What do you mean?"

"I'm trying to tell you this over and over again but you don't listen."

"Then what is it? Say it again then, if I'm that stupid. What is it you want from me? I feel I have given you everything."

"I want your heart."

She looked him straight in the eyes with tears running down her cheeks. Then she looked away, as if she didn't want to show him how much pain she was in.

He had stared at her, feeling as if all air had been struck from his body. He knew he could never give her that, but he couldn't tell her. If he did, he'd have to admit that he had been lying to her the whole time, pretending he could fully love her when in fact a woman had already captured his heart in Rome when he was eighteen. He had met her once again when he was twenty-five, but she had been engaged, and he had then finally given up hope. The love had still been there; he knew, and she had known.

Later Marianne had come into his life, and he had felt they both had something to learn—maybe too much. But they had been together for seven years now. It had never been easy, and he had not always treated her well, he knew that. But she always stayed, and he felt he could show the world that he could be more or less normal when he was with her. His family had been all over the place when he had met her. Finally he was settling down. He had believed in it himself, shutting down his inner voice that was trying to tell him that it was a lie. But he felt he had to go through it. They had been given two kids, not that he had wanted to, but he felt it was the right thing to do. Oskar was now four, and Smilla was two. He was away most of the time, and he knew that Marianne had a lot to do at home. But still—he didn't know what to do with it. He sure as hell was not happy.

A guy on his bicycle was yelling at him at a traffic light, giving him the finger. "Watch where you're driving!"

Michael just looked at him. He had been in his own world while driving, so the guy was right. He said *I'm sorry* with his spread hands.

What a day.

What is that Marianne and I have to learn from each other? What is it that I'm holding on to? I know I can only love Katrin, my Roman woman. I know I have been lucky to meet her twice, but why can't I get it to be right with Marianne, when I'm so clearly now allowed to be with Katrin? What is that I have to learn from Marianne? I know that she is learning a lot from being with me, but what is it that I can't see? Why won't I see it? We are clearly not on the right track. I don't feel I'm on the right track with myself anymore. I want to release that tension in me, that inner tension that just hurts so damn much. What to do? Maybe I should go away for a while.

It had been a long time since he had reflected so honestly about himself. Suddenly it had come to him on this drive to Kristian's. Maybe it had been the closure of that deal, coming across the stupid men, or just knowing that he was about to meet Kristian. They hadn't been alone for a long time, and he knew that Kristian always dared to tell him the truth, not wrapping it up and often also telling him a lot that he didn't really want to hear.

They had met in Copenhagen Business School when they were eighteen years old and had become best friends instantly. It had now lasted for twenty-two years, and they were each other's foundation. Michael didn't like it that Kristian was leaving Denmark now, but he was happy to see how happy he was.

It had been a quite magical meeting when they had met. Michael loved this magic in life. They had quickly found out that they both had been on Roma Termini at the same time that summer when they both had been on Interrail. Kristian had been on his way to Corfu with two of his friends and two women they had met. Michael had been going the opposite direction from Corfu with his brother and their two friends. So they had been so close to meeting, and then they had ended up in the same class three weeks later. It was meant to be. Michael always felt that when life spoke to him in a magical way, he was on the right track. He felt he was listening to the great plan. Some that was just written for him. Lately he had felt that he wasn't on the page anymore—as if he had left his book and become a part of everyone else's books, and he didn't know how to come back to his own, or was he still in his own even if it didn't feel like it?

He had called Kristian in despair after another great argument with Marianne. He needed to see Kristian, he knew that he would give him some new thought constellations that he could use for reflection.

Kristian was the only one who knew about Katrin. He knew that Michael had encountered her at Roma Termini the same day that Kristian had been there. It wasn't often that he had spoken about her; only once, when they had been really pissed in business school, had he confessed that he loved a woman he had never met. It had been a big thing to share that, but it felt great that one person knew it.

Then once again after he had met her in their twenties, when she had been engaged, he had cried in front of Kristian, not knowing what to do.

Kristian had urged him to move on, and he done so, but they both knew that he couldn't do that fully.

Her,
Roman girl,
Was
Always
In him.
What was it
With
Her?
Why
Could his
Heart
Never
Forget her?
How
Could it
Be that
She
Seemed to
Cross
His path?

Seen
And not seen
All the
Time.
His
Pain
Kept
Looping.
When could
He be
Released?
What was
There to be learned?

"Hi, my friend," Michael said.

"Hi."

They gave each other a big hug.

"What do you want to drink?"

"Give me a cappuccino."

"Okay, I'll go and get them."

Kristian came back with two big cups of the black magic.

"So good to see you. Shit, you're going be married soon. How are you feeling?"

"I'm so much looking forward to this, for the first time I feel that I'm getting married because I want to, because I love, because it can't be any different and not because I have to be married to be the right kind of person or all the other programs that we tap into. Do you know what I mean?"

Michael smiled and laughed. "You know I do."

Kristian smiled. "Yes I guess that's why you called. What's going on, Michael? How long have you and Marianne been together?"

"Seven years, and I don't know. Well, that's not exactly true …."

"Thank God you're saying that, because I was just about to tell you that you do know. You just don't want to listen and act."

"I know, but it's just getting worse and worse, and I know I'm a shit in many ways. But I just don't know how to change it. I feel that no matter what I do, it's just not good enough."

"What if you truly listened to yourself, that *knowing* that you're always talking about? The one where you feel that you're on the right page in your book."

"Funny you're saying that. I was just thinking about it on my way here—that I'm just not in my book anymore, and it confuses me. I can't seem to make the right decisions anymore. Only in my work, but I'm starting feeling empty in a way there too. It feels like a major shift. But I'm holding on so much, and I don't know why. What is it with Marianne and me? What is it that I'm holding on to? It's the constant feeling of not being in the right spot, and at the same time I can't move."

"Because if you did, you would be a shithole to her and your whole family, and you don't want that. How can you expect to be in your book on your page if you don't want to listen to what it's telling you?"

"I know."

Michael drifted away and Kristian knew him so well, that he knew he needed time. He thought that Michael often had a funny pace, when it came to his private story and his emotions. He was so slow, but in business and with other people, no one was faster.

"Let it be for now. I need time."

"I know, but it's so good to see you anyway."

"Yes, it is, and I can't wait to see you in Pitigliano and being your best man—again."

"Yes, it's going to be amazing. I can hardly believe it myself, but it feels so right. I now know what you mean when you have been talking about the Roman girl."

"Yeah, it's just that you're to be with yours, and I'm not. By the way, Marianne is not coming. Her sister had booked a holiday for her and Marianne and the kids, so it's just me."

"Maybe that's a good thing. You never know what you'll meet."

Laughter.
Coffee.
Hearts
In
And out
Of love.

Lotte Søs Farran-Lee

The magic
Of life,
The glue,
The inspiration,
Friends,
A wedding,
Italy
And
Love.
Entanglements
That were
Not yet
Discovered.
A script
That had been left.
But could
It ever really
Be left?
Inner lies
Toward a
Truth
That you
Can never
Unscribe.

5

When the Pain Doesn't Leave

"Hi, my dear"

"Hi, Sebastian, how are you? I'm so happy that you had some time today; I've missed you."

"I have missed you too. I'm tired, but good. So much work, but it's really good stuff, so it's okay. And you? How are you?"

"I'm good on the surface but inside—Ahh, shit, Sebastian, it just doesn't leave me …." She had tears in her eyes. She had been here many times before in her life, and Sebastian was always there for her. Like a rock, just not moving, not judging her when the pain of life seemed to be overwhelming.

"What is it that doesn't leave, dear?"

"That pain inside me, it doesn't leave me. I know it has been here all my life, and you know the story about Michael. I met him very briefly in Rome when I was eighteen and then again when I was twenty-five, when I was already engaged to Mads. And that is now eight years since, and I wonder if I did the right thing. I mean I love Mads—he is the best guy in the world, you know that—but that pain, that longing … it just doesn't leave me, and I don't know what to do."

"You've got to go with it. You have to discover the truth about it. You know that I've always said that you should just try to live with it, but you can't. And I know you have done many things in life to try to uncover it. But maybe you know that deep inside you are not completely there."

Katrin looked at him with her big green eyes both wet with tears of sorrow and joy. "Thank you. Do you really mean that?"

"You know I do. I'm always here to support you, but it's so damn hard to see that pain. I know you're doing everything you can; still, I also know you have to put yourself out there. Don't waste your life on not getting it done. And I know you, you can't live halfway. That's why you're in pain."

"You're right, I know that. I'm just so scared, and I'm not used to it. If I get into it I will lose control."

"You're probably right as always. But you got to do it." Sebastian smiled at her.

She smiled back. "Let's order."

"Do you want a menu with sushi, or do you want à la carte?"

"I'll think I'll have the same as usual. Menu B."

"Will happen, and should we have a glass of wine?"

"Yes, absolutely."

"So what are you going to do? Apart from all the therapy that you are discovering."

"I'm thinking about going to a retreat in Greece. Get away a bit and see things from a different angle. I have been going to this therapist for a while, and something is happening, I know, but I think it's better to get away a bit."

"It sounds like a good idea. What does Mads say?"

"He is always cool, you know that. He is a star, and it makes it so damn hard sometimes. I'm so tired of having this pain inside me. Really tired. I feel I have fucked up my soul in a way. I wish that life was a bit simpler."

"You will never be simple. That's what makes you so amazing."

"Thank you, darling."

"Cheers to you! For an exciting trip to Greece, good health, and happy days."

"And cheers to you, too. I hope you're right."

Sushi
and
Wine
Were in
A constant
Flow of enjoyment.
The glasses became
Many,
The laughter
Higher.
To

Lotte Søs Farran-Lee

Pain,
To
Love
For an
Inner
Journey
To
Elaborate.

Katrin had packed her bag, just bringing it all together. It was early June, and she was about to leave for a two-week retreat in Folegandros in Greece. Sebastian and she had had a really good night the other day, and she had felt a change in energy. She hadn't told him that she was in love with her therapist and that something had happened to her inside: she was not in love with him, hoping he would become her boyfriend, but in love with a purpose to understand what love was.

She had fucked up.

She knew that. Something had happened in her plan of getting the projection back, when opening up her heart to him, but it hadn't worked. So now it was not just about the pain in the world anymore, but a pain with her torn soul.

It's such a bad state I've ended up in—being in love with my therapist, when I don't want to be in love with him. I know it's just to get some knowledge, but something has happened inside me. I don't know the track anymore, only that the pain has become more fragile and uncontrolled. I hope this trip can bring me some magic. I hate that I'm so in my own world towards Mads. He is so great, and I feel like I'm a shit. Please give me some clarity, God.

She looked up as if God would hear her more clearly. Her eyes got wet. She took a deep breath and zipped her bag.

"Katri-i-in." Mads was calling her.

"Yes, what's up, honey?"

"Your taxi is here, to take you to Greece."

"Thank you. I'm coming."

"Let me take your bag, I'll walk you to the car."

Katrin looked at him, while he was putting on his trainers. He was such a good man, and they had such an amazing apartment, a good life, and still she could just constantly observe that she was in pain and sad, longing for a life to be unfolded within her. She could get so angry with herself, that she just wasn't happy. She had it all, and yet still she felt she was missing the most important part of her life... *herself.*

The taxi driver stood waiting in the morning mist at the taxi's open door. The streets were completely empty; the city hadn't woken up yet.

Mads was yearning, squeezing her hard. His body told her that she should take care, that he was scared, but that he supported her. She knew his language without him even speaking. He was so scared of losing her, and she couldn't blame him; she felt she had lost herself too.

"Take care, my love."

"Take care, I'll be back soon. Two weeks will pass quicker than you think, and you can finish all the work that's been lying around."

He held her, gently now, looking at her with his mild eyes. "I love you, you know that."

"I love you too. I'm sorry that I'm so confused."

"Don't be. It's okay."

The taxi driver closed the trunk, marking that it was time to go. She pulled herself out of Mads's arms and gave him a soft smile, trying to persuade him that it would be okay.

He wasn't sure.

She neither.

But no one said it out loud.

"I'll miss you."

"I'll miss you, too."

He closed the door. The taxi pulled out and she glanced back. Mads just stood watching the taxi vanishing with her around the corner, not knowing who would come back.

She turned around and glanced out the window. The taxi driver tried to make conversation, but she let it slide, telling him silently that she was not in the mood for talk.

Her mind drifted to thoughts about Mads and their meeting. She had just been twenty-three when they had met. He was five years older than she. They had met each other to a party at the University of Copenhagen. Her longtime friend Louise from boarding school was studying law, and

Mads was in her class. Easy calculation. Katrin had been home on a holiday from her design school in New York, and it hadn't taken that long to recognize the beauty of Mads's being.

It wasn't love at first sight. They just felt a strong connection, and with Katrin in New York, it was a love that slowly blossomed. She liked it that way, and so did he. It wasn't that passionate, but they were good together, good friends and much alike in many ways. Neither wanted children; both worked a lot. The wanted to live in a city and loved travel and eating at fancy restaurants; they might have done that the rest of their lives if not for her constant pain, her soul putting a huge amount of pressure on her to look at that book, that script that was written for her.

Now she was on her way to Greece. First a flight to Athens and a ferry from Piraeus to Folegandros. It was a two-week retreat led by two Danish teachers of yoga and therapy. They were going to be in nature, meditating, eating healthy food, and doing other things she didn't yet have a clue about. She was just open—maybe too open.

Two engines
Speeding up,
Wheels
Lifting,
Reaching
The skies—
Metal in the
Air.
An opening
For a
Soul
To
Find the
Words,
The words
That were
Already
Written
For

Her soul.
It
Felt like
The choices
Were free.
But when
No one listened
To the
Script,
The pain
From the soul
Would
Scream:
"Please listen to
The
Script!"

She landed in Athens and felt the sun's immediate attention when stepping out of the airport. Took herself to Piraeus and found in the chaos the right ferry for the first part to Folegandros. She had some spare time and took a sad Greek salad in a restaurant with all the other travelers to the islands. She was transported by the chaos of people, backpacks, food, dust, oil, and harbor, all mixed up like the salad.

Her thoughts were with her therapist as she desperately tried to figure out what had triggered her soul. She had been awakened in that room with him. She felt she had woken up to who she really was, but what was that? An inner adventure had been kicked off. Mads was worried, and rightly so; she was too. Something had rocked her inner state of being so hard that the page of the script she had been on had been erased, and a new page had not been turned yet.

"Hi, may I sit here with you?"

"Sure."

The woman sat down by her table. She looked European, and Katrin had a feeling that she was going to the same place as her.

"Where are you going?"

"I'm going to Folegandros on a retreat for fourteen days. And you?"

"Me too. I don't know why I had the feeling that you were going too, but it's fun that it's true."

"That's really exciting. What's your name?"

"It's Katrin. I'm from Denmark. And you?"

"I'm Marie, from Sweden."

"So you're with the two o'clock ferry, I presume?"

"Yes, exactly. Have you met others that are going? I think we're going to be ten or twelve people."

"No, I haven't, but I think it was only Scandinavians coming."

"Is it your first time?"

"Yes it is, and you?"

"Yes, it's the same here!"

Two excited
and
Nervous
Women
Traveling
With
An
Inner
Pain
Unfolded their
Conversation
On
A ferry
To Folegandros
And blended
Their
Expectations
Pains
And hopes.

The first week had passed, and the shifts had been many. She felt clean and vulnerable. Every morning she asked to be given a sign for a breakthrough, a breakthrough to her inner knowing.

After morning meditation she went on a walk on her own along the beach. The water was crystal clear, and only sound was the wind.

She had been walking here every day, happy to be on her own, with no emotions to share or processes to witness, just a space of silence. Mads was calling every day, trying to act as though he wasn't affected; it didn't work that well.

She felt she needed peace from him too, but she couldn't blame him for being nervous; she would have been too.

This morning felt different, as if the wind was telling her something. The intensity of it was stronger. She walked further this morning as something in her knew that she needed to walk beyond her comfort zone.

A bit farther down the beach she sees an old man sitting under a tree. She is drawn to him, feeling scared but unable to keep from walking toward him. She thinks it's strange that this man is calling to her with no words, but as if drawn by a magnet she observes her body getting near him.

He has long grey and black hair and holds a stick in his hand. He is wearing a huge black robe that looks like a dress. He has sandals on, and an intensity in his eyes makes her smile awkwardly. He smiles but doesn't say anything. With his right hand he shows her where she should sit.

She follows his gesture and takes a seat on the stone just next to him. He stares at the sea. She copies him, scared to breathe, scared to move … as the hands move on the surface of the clock. She gets into it, relaxes, and stays as if it's the most natural thing in the world to sit with a stranger on a beach overlooking the ocean.

"I have been waiting for you!"

Katrin nearly falls off the stone. She hasn't even considered that they might speak and even less that he can speak English.

He keeps talking, one sentence at a time with long, intense breaks in between. He keeps his eyes focused in the distance, on a spot that only he knows of.

"There is a script for each soul in the sense that events, people, and places are written out for you to experience. All this is what you're longing to experience, because your soul is yearning for you to live its script.

"You're born with your free will on how to live your life, if you want to listen to your script and accept the deal your soul has made for you. The deal is made for you to be sure you receive the lessons you are to learn while here in this body.

"You have the free will to live the script or not. Sometimes the script will not give you free will, and decisions will be made. Other times you can act upon your will, but be alert and sense the difference between being in line and out of line with the script.

"You will find wisdom in that alertness."

Katrin is completely quiet and lets his words take root within her. They find new spots within her, new cracks of awareness where they begin the process of being assimilated.

Katrin breaks the silence. "So what is my script? Is it my soul that is calling me, telling me to live me, since I feel I have fucked up my soul?"

"You can never do that. You can never harm your soul. The worst you can do is not listen to it. Listen to the script, and your soul will be calling for you to wake up. This is what causes pain.

"You will still experience pain even if you live your script, but the pain of not listening is like a constant reminder of pain, that you don't listen. There is a difference.

"Take a look over the ocean. A drawing will appear; that is your assignment. This is your inner pain calling. It's your inner soul of the masculine and feminine to be merged and melted. When you find that wisdom within you, you can truly blossom."

Katrin views the ocean, and as he said, a drawing appears. Without knowing, she knows he is right, and deep within, she knows what she has to do—not knowing that either.

She glances left to take a look at him, only to notice that he is gone. She gets confused, but again not really. He was too mysterious, almost so much that he seemed not to be real ....

"Katrin, Katrin ... wake up. Where have you been? It's lunchtime!"

Katrin heard Marie far away. *What is going on?* "I'm here, I'm awake."

"Are you sure?" Marie was laughing now. "You're lying in the middle of the beach and look like someone who's been knocked down. We were worried about you. You have been away since morning meditation. So we came here to see where you were. Are you all right?"

"So he was just a dream?" Katrin was looking around, truly confused. It hadn't felt like a dream. The old man, the words, the drawing, the wisdom …

It had felt utterly real.

"Who was just a dream, dear Katrin?"

"A wise old man. He told me about the script, my script, and showed me a drawing of my life assignment. Shit, it's so strange. It felt completely real, and now I'm not sure. I can't even remember why I would have fallen asleep here."

"It sounds like a very powerful dream, Katrin. Come on, let's get back. You need some water and some rest."

She
Knew
He had shown
Her the script,
Real or
Not real.
The message was
Clear.
She had to follow that
Script.
No
Way out.
No
Excuses.
The script
Was the only
One.
Michael
Came
Into her
Dreams
That night
Showing her
That he

Lotte Søs Farran-Lee

Was a
Part
Of her
Script.
And she
Was in
His.
It was
Only in
God's
Hands
When
To
Melt!

6

New York

On this Wednesday in April Michael was completely ecstatic. The flight tickets said New York. It was the first time in his life, and he had been looking so much forward to it a great deal. It was better than Christmas Eve when he was a kid, and that said a lot.

Michael was born with two life energy engines, and he loved being in energies that were creative and fast. He loved finding spaces for every opportunity in life to be investigated, and he knew New York would be a space like that. He couldn't wait to get there.

They were the same four who had gone on Interrail seven years ago. It had become a tradition since then. Every year they had gone to different places—Barcelona, London, Prague, Budapest, Berlin, and Paris—but this year they had decided to cross the Atlantic. It was Michael, his brother Lars, Ole, and David.

Lars, David, and Michael had attended the same business school; Ole was still studying art at the university and was completely obsessed with art and design. He was already working part time for a design company. He wanted to have his own business at some point but didn't feel ready yet. Michael, Lars, and David already had an IT business together. They worked nonstop, and they were already very successful. Michael was the creator and Lars the executer, with David handling the finances.

"Are you ready, Michael?" Ole's teasing tone matched the cheeky glint in his eyes.

"Yes, I'm so ready, I can't wait. I have been dreaming about this forever."

"We know."

They were all laughing. Every year Michael had suggested New York, and they had all turned it down for various reason, so they knew how ready he was.

"We have to leave from terminal C. Anyone want a coffee before boarding?"

41

Michael was ahead of them, and they all answered yes. They had their coffee and then boarded the flight. Soon the airplane rose to the skies to take them to JFK New York.

The limousine picked them up in the airport as arranged, and as they drew closer to Manhattan, the excitement between them ramped to higher and higher levels.

They arrived at the Jade Hotel in Greenwich Village, unpacked, and quickly conquered the streets of Manhattan. They were high on the energy of finally arriving. Over a croissant and coffee they discussed how to get the most out of their days here.

Ole had an invitation to a party at a design school Saturday, and everybody agreed to go after a nice dinner. Central Park, Wall Street, Fifth Avenue, the Guggenheim, the Empire State Building, and then all the galleries and of course food, wine, and coffee were on the list. They were all single and ready to get the New York adventure started.

"Katrin, are you coming to the party Saturday?"

Her Italian roommate Milo poured two cups of coffee for them in their tiny kitchen. It was small but so cozy, with high windows and a mixture of Italian and Danish styles. All three of them were studying at the design school here in Manhattan. The third roommate, Debra, was from Ohio. They were quite different, but that had turned out to be a strong asset.

"I'm not sure. I have an assignment that needs to be done by Monday, and I'm way behind. What day is today?"

"It's Wednesday, so you do have a couple of days to go."

"Yes, it could be fun."

"Yes, it could, and what about just a couple of hours? You could just have one drink, and you haven't been out almost for two months now."

"You know it's been crazy. So much work at school and then the engagement with Mads, I can't believe it. I'm twenty-five, and I'm engaged."

She was still sitting in the kitchen in her pajamas, writing and listening to some nice jazz. She looked at the rock on the finger. She couldn't believe it. He had actually proposed to her last month when he was here. They had gone out for lunch, and then on a bench in the middle of Central Park, he went down on his knees and proposed, without any warning whatsoever.

They didn't even live in the same country, but Mads just felt it was right, and she didn't feel like saying no.

Milo said, "Yes, it's crazy, but you are crazy, and it would be so great if you came. You need it."

"Milo, Milo, you're right. I'll let you know tomorrow morning, okay?"

"It's a deal, Bella. And here's your coffee."

"Thank you. What are you doing today, Milo? I thought of going to the park later. Do you want to join me?"

"Sounds like a brilliant idea."

"I'll be back at two, okay?"

"That's beautiful."

"Ciao, bella."

"Ciao, ciao!"

Her
Head
Was in
The face
Of the computer
Absorbed
By the letters,
The
Combination
That would lead
Them to
Understanding.
That
Was easy.
What was not
Was the understanding
Of events
That kept looping
In life
Telling a
Story
That no one could

Control.
The story
Called
Life.

"Are you ready Michael?"

"We're leaving now."

"Yes, I'm ready. I'll meet you in the hall."

Damn, I'm always late, but I just have to get this finished. So many great ideas are coming here in NY. It's like my soul is being fed from deep within. Ahh, I miss some people who get that side of me. It's just Grandpapa who knows that side of me. It's a bit exhausting to be on the beat all the time, when my soul is not being fed, but how and where can I share that? Please send me a sign that something magic is truly right in the world; send someone who will make it sparkle.

He glanced at himself in the mirror, satisfied with what he saw. He was wearing a slimcut shirt and blazer and was clearly in good shape. Time to leave. He had a look around in the hotel room, switched off the light, closed the door, and went to the elevator.

"So where are we heading?"

"We have booked a table at a sushi restaurant near the design school, and then we're going to attend the party at around ten."

"Excellent. I'm up for a party tonight."

"Ole, was it you who knew someone there?"

"Yes, my mentor from the school has a close colleague here, and he said we could join the party and I could have a small talk with him. He might be good for my future and have good connections here."

"Excellent again."

Michael was in a brilliant mood, and they were all laughing. They were ready to knock down the city tonight.

A prayer
Had been
Sent.
Was the prayer

To be heard?
And if it did
Was it
His creation?
What prayer
Was to be answered,
And whose was not?
Had that
Already been
Written in
The script
too?

"Shit, you look damn sexy, Katrin. I'm so happy you could come."

"Thanks, Matt. You don't look too bad either."

"It's a pity you're getting married; otherwise we would have made a great one."

Katrin laughed out loud. She was literally sparkling in her silver sequined dress and deep red lips.

"You're so cute, Matt. Where are the drinks?"

"I'll show you."

He laid a hand on her back while pointing in the direction of the bar. She and Matt were chatting away about life. He thought he was the center of the world, and although he was being a bit obnoxious, he was kind of cute in his own way. Katrin was glancing across the bar when she noticed four handsome men at the end of the bar. They didn't look familiar to her; they were not from this school, and they seemed in some way inquisitive. She looked at Matt and absently carried on the conversation while clutching her drink, playing with the straw, and glancing toward the four men again. They definitely had her attention in a secret way.

She looked back at Matt and replied to his ongoing speech about the ideas he would implement in life when he was done with the school. It got a bit boring, but Matt seemed not to notice her lack of full attention.

She looked at the group again, and this time a pair of eyes met hers. She almost dropped her drink, flushed hot, and simply couldn't take her eyes off his.

He smiled.
She smiled.
An intense
Eye contact
Was kept.
A prayer had been
Heard.
The owner
Of the prayer
Had no idea
That a
Special one
Had
Just
Arrived;
Only his
Soul
Knew.

"Katrin, where are you? You're not listening to me. Looks like some guy is stealing your attention. Remember, you're engaged."

"I'm sorry, Matt. I think I know this guy, but I'm not sure from where."

"I think he is interested in you too. He keeps staring."

Katrin looked back at him and smiled again. *Where have I seen those eyes before? It's like they know me deep within.*

"Maybe you should talk to him. It looks like he can't take his eyes off you."

"No, I don't want to do that. I have Mads."

"Yes, but you can still talk to me. Hence you can talk to that guy too."

"Sure, Matt, you're right. —No I'm going to leave it."

But her eyes kept wandering back to his eyes. She couldn't get enough, and she felt she was stealing small moments of contact between their eyes.

Matt had moved on, and she stood a moment on her own, sensing the ambience and sipping her drink, when the guy came over.

"Hi!"

"Hi." She sank into herself one more time.

The eyes were close to her now. She just smiled, and he smiled back. The silence was a beautiful one, the kind where everything just seemed right.

"What's your name?"

"Katrin, and yours?"

"It's Michael."

"I must say I feel I've seen you before, but I just don't know where."

"Me too. Are you from here?"

"Well, I'm studying here, but I'm actually from Denmark. And you?"

"I'm from Denmark too. I'm just on a holiday, and one of my friends knows a teacher here, so we were invited. It's unbelievable that you are from Denmark too. Have we met before?"

"I have no idea, but there is something very familiar."

"Mmmm, I know. Do you want a drink?"

"Yes, that would be kind of you."

"What do you like?"

"A GT is always a safe choice."

Michael laughed. "Yes, you're right about that. I'll get it for you."

He went to the bar to get some drinks, glancing over at his friends. They had urged him to go over to Katrin when they saw he couldn't take his eyes off her. Now they smiled very smoky eyes back. He replied with a "mind your own business" look.

His friends had left
They had been talking and talking
The words wouldn't stop
It was synchronicity
On a higher
Level.
A level higher
Than they could
Image.
It felt like an eternity.
They had
Left the party,
Gone for a walk,

One that
No one
Wanted to end.
The hours had
Become many.
It said six
O'clock in the morning
When they split.
Everything was
Magic.
Everything was
Spot on.
They both knew.
Only one
Detail.
She was to get married.
They both knew
Timing was
Not right.
But the pain and
Suffering had
Hit them both.
Although neither
Said it out loud,
For a moment
Two souls
Had felt at home
More than ever.

Why, God? Why are you doing this to me? What have I done to you? Are you joking with me? This was the most amazing thing in my life, and now she is getting married. And I just can't take it. It was everything, she *was everything. My pain stopped; my longing stopped. It was* her, *and you know it.*

Michael was swearing silently. They had parted at the Starbucks coffee shop near her home. He was now on his way back to their hotel. And he was angry with life more than he had ever been.

Lotte Søs Farran-Lee

Suddenly, when the thought came that *it was* her, *and you know it*, he understood who she was. She was *the one* from Roma Termini. He had met her again and hadn't really understood until now. She was the special one, he knew, the one his soul he had been longing for, and now again she was gone.

She hadn't wanted to exchange numbers. She was about to get married, and it was too much. She had said that she hoped their ways would cross again, but life had to show it to them. She knew it was special, but she couldn't choose differently now.

The goodbye had been awful. It had torn his soul to see her leaving with moist eyes wide. He had kissed her on both cheeks, and they had hugged for a long time. Time had to tell the story, but damn, it hurt, more than he had ever known before.

He looked into the heavens and cried out, "Why, God? Why?"

The answer was silence. He knew that in time the knowing would come, as always, but right now everything felt black.

That night, he decided that the greater belief was bullshit and turned off the listening to his inner voice. It was the only way he would survive the pain of not being with her.

She had run after she turned the first corner, only to try get the pain out of her body, while the tears were running down her cheeks. What an irony. She was about to get married, and then *he* showed up. Who was he? She felt his eyes piercing into her soul over and over again.

Where have I seen you before? Why does it feel that every time I meet you, you have to leave? When are we going to be together? Are we ever going to be together? I know I have to go through this with Mads, I just know it. But why does it hurt so much? Who are you?

Then in a flashback, she saw his face, his eyes, at Roma Termini. What was going on? Could it be? Yes. Damn, it was *him* from Rome, and she didn't want him in her life right now. She had been dreaming about him for seven years, and now she had turned him down. *Shit, Katrin!*

But she knew she had to follow this. There was a greater meaning with this, but that didn't diminish the pain.

What they had thought was a first time
Meeting
Was wrong.
Two souls were in pain,
A pain that was in the script.
Their souls
Were to grow
And for them
The deal
Was time
With uncertainty
And unknowing,
Learning to
Trust the
Inner knowing
That they
Were in
The same script.
Only it was
Written
In a way
That they did not
Agree
Upon.

Lars, David, and Ole had been quiet all day, handling him with care. For the first time he felt they understood him when he was in pain. They could see the suffering that had entered his life after last night. He hadn't slept all night. It had been magic with Katrin, and all of them were baffled over the fact that it had been *her* from Roma Termini seven years ago. She had shown up here in New York, and they had the same impact on each other ... and then came the devastating news that she was getting married.

Michael was completely heartbroken, and she hadn't even left him a phone number. She didn't want to be in touch—the pain would be too hard on them both, and she was probably right. But why? Why didn't she choose differently if she could see how great they were together, how special it was?

Michael had gone for a walk on his own while the others paid a last visit to a museum. They were to depart late that evening.

He went down to the Hudson River and relished the wind in his face, wishing it to sweep away all the pain.

He desperately wanted to make sense of it, but nothing came. Nothing. Just this immense pain of not understanding and a feeling of being let off the track from what he really wanted. A place where he just felt he belonged.

A long night,
A place where everything
Was
The most pure and magical
He
Had
Ever
Felt.
It was gone.
It felt like it would be forever.
No logic
Nothing to do
Nothing to say
Just to accept.
He needed a place,
A place
To escape,
Shutting
Down
To that voice
That
He had
Always trusted.
He left
New York

With friends
With a shattered
Heart
And a will that
It should never
Be hurt again.
Closed
The sense
Of being true
To
The script.

7

Granddad

"Granddad, Granddad."

"Yes, Michael. What's up, my dear?"

"Look what I found."

"Let me see."

Michael's granddad sat down and closely examined what Michael had found. Michael was an energetic child, always talking, finding stuff, running around all the time, and not that easy to control, but his granddad could just by his breath make Michael quiet. So Michael didn't say a word while his granddad was investigating the stone Michael held so proudly in his hand.

"Ahh, it's so beautiful, Michael. Where did you find it?"

"I found it just down by the water. I could just see it. It looked like a heart."

"Yes, it sure does. It's amazing that you found exactly that one. Did you know, Michael, that stones are alive too?"

"How, Granddad? How? It looks dead to me."

"Well, for it to take one breath can take up to two thousand years."

"Wow, Granddad, is everything really alive?"

"Yes, it is. Everything is energy, my boy."

Michael and his granddad were walking along the beach, it was a bit rough and windy this autumn day, but they didn't care. This was their day. Every Saturday Michael's granddad would pick him up, and they would go somewhere, mostly nature, where they would walk and talk. They had their routines: they always had to have the hot chocolate that Granddad brought and biscuits. Later they would eat the same sandwiches, one with ham and one with egg and mayo. Every Saturday it was the same.

Michael loved these days. They had followed this routine since he was four, and now, three years later it was the same. Michael's mom and dad had asked Granddad if he wanted to, and he had promptly replied with a positive answer. Michael could become really intense for the whole family, and often he asked questions about life that they had no answers to. Granddad did; he was a wise man and hence Michael was over the top of joy when Granddad's red little car arrived to take him out of the house.

Michael felt that Granddad knew everything in life, and Granddad saw and understood that Michael was not like most kids. He had very complex questions; he wanted to understand completely how things came about and was never satisfied with a simple answer.

Granddad knew that Michael observed life differently than most children, but he didn't make any fuss about it. Irene, his daughter, had asked him to take Michael every Saturday, and it had felt so natural to him to spend his Saturdays with Michael. He loved it himself. He had also had a granddad that had spent a lot of time with him, teaching him the exact same wisdom—the simplicity and complexity of life, hand in hand. Granddad was there.

"Come, Michael, we have to go home now."

"Why, Granddad? I want to stay."

"But it's time to go to Granddad's; it's dinnertime."

"Are we having the same?"

"Yes we are, my boy."

"Woohoo!" Michael was running and dancing.

The dinner was not spectacular, but it was Michael's favorite meal of the week. Boiled carrots, a steak, Béarnaise sauce, and water were the ingredients. Every Saturday it was the same. Granddad knew what Michael loved, and he was willing to offer that. Irene and Torben were not willing to give Michael a tight schedule, which would have made him more restless. He would pick on them too much, but they knew what his meaning was on that subject.

After dinner they played cards, and then Granddad went out to have his pipe while Michael was watching TV. Then his teeth were brushed and pajamas buttoned, and Granddad read the same book until Michael had entered the world of dreams.

Granddad
Was his everything—
His anchor,
His guidance,
His understanding,
His rock.
It was that place
In the world
Where he felt
The safest,
The place where
Everything was
Good.
He
Felt
Loved.
He learned
He was.

Michael was on his way to a date. He had tried to date many times after his trip to New York, but now three years later he was still single. It was hopeless; he always ended up being an asshole, and it wasn't the women's fault. They all just had one major problem: they were not Katrin.

Still, he just really wanted to share life with someone. Mostly the sex was okay, and maybe he lasted a couple of dates, but then they wanted him to commit, and he just couldn't, so he ran like a fool. He wouldn't answer their calls, couldn't wrap it up with good style. He hated this, but it just kept happening.

He worked his ass off. He, Lars, and David had really created a luxury business, amassing lots of money into their bank accounts. They all had the right addresses, the right clothes, and the right cars. David was already married and Lars soon to go. Michael was the only bachelor left.

It had been so strong this night. It was like she was sleeping next to me. Why do I keep having these dreams, if she is not to be with me? I'm going crazy, and now again, I'm trying to go on a date, and I don't even want to. I just want it to go away with Katrin, so I could meet someone else.

He had nearly called her a couple of times since New York. He had found her on the internet and had found her number. But he couldn't; she had said she wouldn't, and he felt too anxious to call her. Maybe she would reject him, and he just couldn't bear that pain.

What the fuck am I doing? I don't want to go on this date. I have to cancel now. I know I'm an asshole, so what the fuck! Or should I call? Ah shit, I'll text her. I have to leave with Granddad to Sicily tomorrow anyway, so it doesn't make sense. I know it's a bad excuse, but I just have to stop it.

The text
Was short;
The message
Was clear.
He was not
To be
With her
At the restaurant.
He turned his car
And drove
With his frustration,
His longing,
His loss.

"Hi Granddad. Can I come now?"

"Sure, but weren't you supposed to come early tomorrow morning?"

"Yes, but I cancelled my meeting. It didn't feel right."

"Come, my boy."

They both hung up. Michael headed toward Granddad's house. He already had his suitcase packed in the car. He'd been sure he could have stayed with her for the night. Plans had changed, and it felt better this way. He knew Granddad knew that he had cancelled a date, but he was too noble to mention it.

He knew that Granddad was getting older, so he'd invited him to

Sicily. He had rented a car and a house with a pool. The pool was for Michael.

They both loved good food and books and small trips, so Sicily was perfect spot for them.

"Hi, Michael, so good to see you. How are you, my boy?"

Michael didn't say anything. He just looked deeply into Granddad's eyes. Granddad knew he was suffering. He knew about the loss of Katrin and his desperation of trying to find a substitute.

Granddad hugged him really hard and held on. Michael let his breath go deeper in Granddad's arms, longer that he had done in a long time.

"Have you packed, Michael?"

"Yes, I've got everything with me. I just changed plans on where to sleep."

"I know. Come and have a glass of scotch with me by the fire."

"That sounds brilliant."

The sound of the silence
Was breaking
And in that crack
Was
Grief
And sadness
To be expressed
In a
Nonverbal
Communication.
The light of
The fire,
The scotch
Burning in the throat.
The silence
Of two
Souls
One holding the other
While in pain.
An understanding

For the other one
To
Be
With
The feeling
Of not being
On the
Right
Track.

8

Moving On

He parked the car. It was a cold dark night. The velvet of snow covered the landscape. Lars's and Lis's house was full of twinkle lights. It looked like a fairytale evening. Not a wind, only the crunch of shoes moving in the frozen snow. He pulled the collar of his coat tight to his neck and ears. He had just arrived home from Iceland, and even if it was much colder there, he found the cold in Denmark much harder to handle. He hated winter; mild summer was more his feeling.

Iceland had been great. He had been there with one of his friends, Anja; they had become very good friends when working for a client. He liked her raw business attitude; she had a solid business network, and she was good for his career. He knew that she had a bit of a crush on him, but a lot of his female friends did that. He used it for his own good, but he also knew it would never become serious, so he didn't care that much about it. They would have to deal with it themselves. He liked being friends with women, they had a softer view on life.

He loved doing business and creating the visions for their projects, but it was Lars and David who executed it with their thorough and straightforward style. Michael loved being the creator, and he was brilliant at it. He could see things coming into fashion before others did, and it was a huge advantage for them all when creating their business.

Anja and he had been in Iceland to visit some potential customers and had then taken a couple of days to make a nature adventure out of it. It had been so amazing, Anja had a friend from Iceland who had taken them around in the landscape. They had seen the most amazing nature he had ever experienced, and they had been in all the outdoor Jacuzzis and hot springs they had passed. It was an amazing feeling sitting in the dark nights in this really cold weather and then being filled with the heat from the water. They had become drunk a couple of nights and had some good talks on life. He knew she had hoped for a kiss, but he had softly avoided it, so it wouldn't become awkward.

He had had some quiet moments for himself too. He needed that sometimes to get away, and it was nice with some sort of company, like Anja, where he could escape from time to time to get deeper into his own quietness. He had closed down a special part of his inner truth after Katrin; it was too hurtful to get in there, and he was scared that life could never be as fine as when he had been with her. He had always thought that if he just lived from that magical place, everything would work out, but it had felt as though the voice had lied to him, when Katrin had been there the second time and then was to be married. It had been seven years now.

He had become more aware of that voice, but he didn't trust it as much as he used to; he feared that it would hurt him.

One day in Iceland he had gone for a walk on his own, when they had been in a nature park. He was absorbing the wild nature, the roughness and the deep frequency he felt from the earth. It was vibrating deeply within him. He had asked for an answer to the tiredness and insecurity of being alone so much. He wanted to grow, to expand, to be greater all the time, and he felt stuck. What if life could never be magical again? What if his expectations of life were too high?

Why?
What?
When?
And how?
Can I change this for me?
I need to forget the longing in my soul!
I need to move on!
I want to!
I want to control it!
I'm so tired of feeling lost in a love that is so great.
I'm a fool.
A fool in love.
But I'm alone
And stuck.
I just need to find someone to

Be with.
Maybe not that great love
But love.

He hadn't felt that he'd gotten an answer being in silence with himself, but he felt that he finally needed to move on. He was mainly angry at himself because he felt he'd settled for second best, and he hated that.

"Hi, Michael. I'm so glad you could come."

"Hi, Lis. It's so good to be here, and these flowers are for you."

"Ahh—thank you. Just let yourself into the living room. They are waiting for you." She gave him a cheeky smile; he was, as always late. He smiled back as if to say *I know, but that's me.*

Lars and Lis had invited him for dinner with several friends. They had just bought a spectacular house and were going for a housewarming just as spectacular. He had forgotten to bring a gift, but Lars and Lis were used to that, so at the last minute he bought her a bouquet with a price tag on.

He entered the room, took a glass of champagne from the golden tray and greeted everyone. He knew most of them, but one women was new. She wasn't stunning, but she had nice features: curly blond hair and nice round breasts. She was a bit withdrawn with her sweet little smile. Despite her very red lipstick, she was shy and mild. Her name was Marianne.

For dinner
They had lamb.
At the table
A conversation
Took place.
No magic
But enough
For some to grow.
She was there
Holding his back;
He was not satisfied
But okay.
He was
Happy.

For a
Moment
He had peace,
Peace in his life—
No one to pressure him
For being single.
He hoped it could
Last.
Not thinking about it.
He made a deal with himself.
It had to last.
With time
He forgot
To treat her rightly—
Selfishness
Always
A deep inner anger
That she wasn't *her.*
But he wouldn't accept it.
Couldn't accept it.
Wouldn't listen.
Fighting for the normality of life
To be,
To stay.

With time he started to enjoy being the one who had it all. He was no longer the last single who didn't have a relationship.

He felt normal. He loved to play the game of being normal, and Marianne, with her sweetness and down-to-earth approach, made it really easy. He even fell in love with the whole scenery of being normal. Children came quickly, and Marianne took care of the house and the foundation. He worked a lot, traveled a lot, and wasn't very present with them.

But they were there as a part of the whole beautiful picture of a successful businessman with a house and a kind of a wife, even though they were not married, and kids. It was good. He had found that station where he could be. He had never really settled for less, and in a way Marianne would probably always be that—be less than Katrin—but Katrin was not here. She was married, and he had to move on … and so he had.

Marianne was a really kind woman, not hot but nice. In the beginning she had just accepted everything that he wanted to do. He really liked it; it was as if he could be single again and then have it all. He sometimes wished that she had a bit more confidence and power, but on the other hand he liked that she just said yes to everything he wanted to do, and then she took care of the base.

He was happy.
Happy with the setup.
He had shut down that *voice*,
That voice
That told him the truth,
The truth about him.
He didn't want to hear.
He thought he was in control,
Control of how his life could be.
He just didn't know
That life
Had a
Different plan.

9

The Pink Bike

Katrin sat in her morning meditation.

It had been her regular routine since Greece more than seven years ago, ever since she had fucked up her soul. She was now forty, single, and in really good shape. She had been on a long soul search for many years and had felt completed when leaving Rome and the Italian Angel. She felt that she knew and had dared to learn how to learn to love unconditionally. She just felt that there was something more her soul hadn't experienced yet.

Feel your breath …. Feel how your body is moving when breathing in and out. Relax, Katrin. Yes, but I want to go to that party …. Just breathe, Katrin, breathe. Maybe I should wear that pink dress instead of the black one? Breathe, Katrin, feel it now. Feel your breath.

In her meditation Katrin was fighting her inner thoughts to be present, to be. Some days it worked; others were a disaster. The days when the focus was strong on an intention or an unknown matter to be resolved were the days when she could barely focus. She sat in her apartment with a view of the harbor. She lived in a luxury flat; it wasn't that big, but it was so well organized that it seemed bigger. In the corner of the living room she had arranged a secret space for herself with a meditation pillow on the floor, candles, a Buddha sculpture, and incense. The view was spectacular today. The sun had just found its first presence above the horizon in the distance. She took a deep breath, absorbing the beauty of the water, the silence, and the silhouettes of the trees, blinded by the sun.

Breathe, Katrin. Stay with it; feel your tummy, feel yourself getting heavier and heavier. Ahh, you're just trying to persuade yourself that you are there in the zone. You know you'll never get there today. I know, but still the twenty minutes is not done yet. Breathe, Katrin, breathe. Jesus Christ, you're so stubborn today. Breathe, Katrin, breathe ….

She sighed deeply. Knew it would never be a day for the deep insights.

Her intention was strong; she felt happy, her fucked-up situation in life was gone, but the emptiness of a completion was hanging in her body. She wanted to move, she wanted to share—she wanted to make love. The separation from Mads had been mild, and they had landed in a spot where it all could shift. The part of having no children had of course made it easier.

"Hi, Rikke."

"Hi, my love."

"I'm on my way now."

"That's so great. I'm just cooking for us."

"What are we having?"

"Uh, I'm doing a very tender chicken with salvia, a delicious salad, and a beautiful Pinot Noir."

"Mmmm, that sounds great."

"Where are you?"

"I'm just on my bike around Sortedam Dossering. So I will be at your place in ten or fifteen minutes."

"Wonderful, darling."

"Is anyone else coming?"

"Yes, a work colleague of mine, Liv."

"Beautiful. See you soon."

"Bye, love."

"Bye."

She grabbed her pink bike. It was hideous but she loved it. It had been her dream since childhood to have her very own pink bike. She was probably a bit too old for this style, but she didn't give a shit.

The day was magical, it had been like that all day long. The sun had been mild and warm with no wind and a temperature above twenty-five degrees. She had gone for a walk after meditation and breakfast along the wharf and had gone for her favorite café near Nyhavn to drink a perfectly brewed cappuccino. She had read almost a whole novel in the sun and felt relaxed and at peace with herself when walking back home. She had taken a quick shower and had changed to a light summer dress with her flip-flops and sunglasses and left the building on her pink bike towards Rikke.

Buzz—
The doorbell
Rang.
Three bips—
Rikke:
"Come up."
Ran the stairs.
Met the two.
Ate
Drank.
Most of the last.
Crashed in
The late hours
Of the morning.
Hammered
And
Happy.

The morning revealed itself with its shadows from the early morning sun. Katrin went to the toilet and was in a daze, half-sleeping and half-awakening. She went back to her spot on the sofa that had carried her through the night and went back to the sense of half sleeping.

"Hi, Katrin."

What was that? First she thought it was Rikke, but then she saw the old man from Greece again. She had tried to ask for his presence since Greece, but it had never happened—and now he was before her in Rikke's living room.

"Hi. I have been trying to ask for your presence for a long time."

"I know, I have been hearing you."

"But why haven't you arrived then?"

Katrin was a bit annoyed with him, that he was the one in charge for them to meet; it had been the same with Angelo, the Italian Angel. She was tired of all those who she felt controlled her.

"It hasn't been the right time yet. You had a lot of learning to absorb."

"I know, but you gave me that strong picture, and I got a lot of other clues from my Italian Angel to learn, but why haven't you been around? I still have this feeling that the picture you gave me is not completed—and I need help!"

"That's why I'm here now. You're right that your Italian Angel … Angelo helped you to learn how to love unconditionally, and now you're ready to unite."

"Yes, I know. Something is missing, but I feel I have had the time to breathe. I have felt all the time that there is a man that I can be with, fully, melt with, like you showed me."

"And there is. It's time for you to meet."

She had asked for his presence since Greece. She never knew if she was dreaming, talking to herself, or if it was real. She just knew that the information had a character that was so important for her life that she couldn't ignore the information. Then in the end it didn't matter where it came from.

A meeting at a café in the middle of Copenhagen. She is sitting in front of a man; it's him. She knows. It's him, the one she has felt the whole time would show up in her life. The one she can melt with. The physical presence of the energy that she knows is real between a man and a woman. She takes a deeper look at him. He has nice brown eyes with a deep warmth and wisdom within. His face is round, and his dark hair doesn't look that Scandinavian. He smiles. They talk. He is a businessman, he has money, his name is Michael …. Information is arriving like a sushi on a running conveyer belt. It's him, I know, I know … he is coming now.

Katrin woke up with a sudden jerk on Rikke's sofa. Had she been dreaming or sleeping, or was it real? The old man had been here too, and he had shown her the man, the man she had known all the time existed.

What time is it? It's only eight o'clock, and we didn't go to bed until four a.m. Wow, he is coming, I just know now. But I feel I have seen him before, and the name …. Ahh, I had too much to drink. I'm too slow. But he is coming, finally, after all these years of searching. I need a cup of coffee … and I need to pee.

Katrin turned herself slowly on one side, folded the underpants out from between her buttocks while she stretched her whole body. Her hair was a mess, and her breath was bad. She took a deep breath, yawned, and sat and stared out into the living room, which was full of empty bottles, old records they had played, and half-burned candles. It had been a fantastic evening, they had addressed everything they could possible think of. It had just been so much fun. Rikke was a golden star in her life, a rock.

Slowly Katrin moved her body to the kitchen, glancing though the door to Rikke's bedroom to see her still sleeping. Turned her attention to the boiler and prepared the coffee. She yawned again and stretched, went to the bathroom, and brushed her teeth. Studied herself with an intense look into her own eyes and smiled.

He is coming Katrin, he is coming now. Finally after all these years, he will show up. I know it! I can't wait to tell Rikke about it. All my work is paying off now.

The smell of the fresh brewed coffee woke her senses, and she gave herself the golden drops.

"Morning, my beauty."

"Morning, Rikke, did you sleep well?"

"Yes, I did. What a wonderful evening. It's been a long time since we just hung out like that."

"Yes, it has been. Why does it take us so long to have these evenings, when they are so great?"

"What time is it?"

"It's eight o'clock."

"Really! Are you mad, Katrin? Then I'll need to sleep some more."

"I know, I feel the same, but I woke up with a very weird but very real dream. So I just had to get up. Sorry that I woke you up."

"Don't worry. Did you make some coffee?"

"Yes, sure. I'll fix you a cup."

"Thanks."

Rikke laughed as she walked naked to the toilet. Katrin smiled at the glimpse of her nakedness. Rikke had always been such a free spirit, and she never delayed any outcome of her thoughts. They arrived instantly, to the annoyance of many. Katrin thought it was liberating and fun, and she always turned to Rikke when she needed the truth in a raw, uncut version.

Katrin sighed, took a sip of her coffee, and stared into nothingness. She was tired yet also excited. She loved when she received messages like this; she knew they were important and true. He was coming now!—the man she could melt with, the place where her soul longed to be. It was her life purpose, to melt with him. She had always hoped that she could be like all the others, longing for the same things as they did, but she didn't, she knew. She longed to be with a specific soul, and she knew it was her purpose to bring herself to that state where she could receive him fully. It was her journey. Her pain was mostly that it was a lonely ride and that no one could fully understand, even herself. She often thought it didn't made sense in any way, but every time she tried to walk away from that part, that longing, she felt miserable.

From her logical side, she couldn't see how she could make it. How could it happen? How could it manifest? When it would happen? Why had she been given this journey? So many whys, hows, and whens …. Time had taught her that her greatest lesson was to let go of the hows and the whens.

It just wasn't that easy.

"You look awfully fresh, how can that be?"

Rikke came to where she sat and gave her a kiss on the head, while her soft breasts gently touched her naked arm.

Katrin couldn't help laughing. "Sorry, sweetheart, but your breast is almost in my coffee—and yes I'm quite fresh. I had a wonderful message this morning."

Rikke looked up with a sudden intensity, still chuckling over the breast-in-the-coffee thing. "Like when you get these messages about the future?"

"Yes."

"Hmmm, what was it about?" Rikke was suddenly much fresher and more alert.

"He is coming."

"Who is coming?"

"The man that I have known would come."

"What do you mean? You know me, Katrin. I don't get it like you do. Please, spell it out for me."

"Well, the old man that I told you about—the guy I saw or dreamt about in Greece, the man who is giving me the messages. He came this morning again. Like in a dream again, but not in a dream …. Anyway, that's quite difficult to explain. But he showed me *him*. He showed me that man I'm going to melt with, and I feel I have seen him before, and his name is Michael …."

"You're crazy, you know that, my dear. But that is so great to hear. Isn't it the same name as the dear Michael you met when you were eighteen in Rome and twenty-five in New York?"

Rikke took a sip of her coffee and watched her dear friend's face changing. Suddenly was no longer excitedly telling a story but had just found out she had won the lottery.

"You … what did you say?"

"Isn't it the same name as the guy you used to talk about? The guy you met at Roma Termini and then later in New York when you were to marry Mads? It must have been like fifteen years ago—"

"You're right, it's him. God damn it, it's him! How could I not see that straight away?"

"You're crazy, Katrin … but I love you!" Rikke smiled at Katrin. She knew that it would come true with this Michael. Katrin had this weird sense of manifesting the strangest and most magical things in life, events and happenings that for almost all others were unattainable … but not for Katrin, and even if she struggled with her belief and pain in life for being different, she always manifested her visions … the visions that were given her. And this time from an old man.

Katrin smiled at Rikke. "You know it's gonna happen!"

"Yes, I know, Katrin. You just have to stay with your belief."

"I know, that's the one where I always get shattered."

"But don't walk away from it. You know it's true in the end anyway. Trust that weird sixth sense you have. It's so powerful. It's only yourself that takes you down all the time. Stop it. You know it's true."

"I know. I know it so deep within my heart. It's my path to melt with him. It's just me that constantly is trying to get away from it, because I don't think it's something worthy. I wanted to have a different path, even though I think it's so beautiful and I feel so happy. I just still wish that I was the postman, but then again … I don't."

"You just have to go with it. Go with your heart, like you have always done."

"I know." Katrin spaced out for a bit, staring out in the space that contained so many possibilities and some that seemed to be already written.

Rikke emptied her cup and took Katrin into her arms and kissed her on the top of her head. "I'm tired and I will go and hug my duvet some more. I'm greatly missed."

Laughter,
Friends,
Understanding,
And love.
So much love.
The meeting ended.
Katrin
Left.
Took her
Pink bike
And let it
Carry
Her
All
The way
Home.
A cup
Was made.
It was
Full of
Tea.
Her ass
In the seat
Of her sofa.

Reflections on the day kept running and sorting themselves out in the part of the brain where bliss was found. Her mind kept reflecting on the script as what was already written and to be surrendered into—and what was free will? The space in the universe seemed to have a wisdom that she couldn't grasp with her intelligence; only the wisdom of her heart knew that something was written out for her and that man Michael that could not be erased. It was just a matter of how and when, but that she had no control of either.

10

A Wedding

"Katri-i-in, we are here!"

Katrin turned and saw Sebastian and Stine at the café. The terminal was full of people, so it was no wonder that they weren't that easy to see.

"Hi, I'm coming over."

They were laughing. It was a genuine mess today; it looked as if a whole football tournament was about to depart from Copenhagen. Finally she got through the chaos of people and reached her friends.

"Thank God that we don't have to check in today."

"Should we move?

"Yes, Sebastian, let's do that."

"Do you need to buy anything in tax-free?"

"Nope, I'm all good."

"Super. Let's go, Bella."

It had been a long time since she had been out of the country. After all the traveling she had done when she had fucked up her soul, she had felt the need to stay home in Denmark and just be, and so she had. She had never felt at home in Denmark before, but meeting herself had been a life changer.

Still, being back in the airplane seat felt so good.

"So what do you want to see in Rome?" Katrin asked.

"Everything."

"Well, it's not that complicated to get around in Rome, so with two whole days, we can see a lot. Have you been there before, Stine?"

"No, I haven't, so I'm dying to get there and see all the beautiful buildings and have a cappuccino. Sebastian, you have been there, right?"

"Yes, but that was when I was a child, so I don't recall anything particularly. But I would love to get some good wine and food."

"Well, that won't be a problem, you'll see."

"Is it weird going back, Katrin?"

"Well, both yes and no. Yes because it's been a while since I was there, and it was so intense when I was traveling a lot—and no because I feel I'm going home to a special part of me. I'll know when we get there."

Katrin started to show them the map of Rome with all the possible sights and destinations. She knew it by heart from the many times she had wandered the city, and it was great to finally show Sebastian and Stine her Rome. They had two days there, and then on Friday they would drive to Pitigliano to attend Kristian's and Giovanna's wedding the next day. They were all excited, and Katrin knew from Sebastian that Kristian was beyond happy. He and Giovanna were going to live in her apartment in the Monte Verde section of Rome. She had a wonderful roof apartment with a terrace. Kristian would open up an office in Rome to do his business from there.

They had rented a car. Stine was not very keen on that, but they would have much more freedom, and Katrin had guaranteed them that she was skilled in Italian driving. They had rented a hotel south of the center of Rome. So everything was set, ready to go.

Once
Again
Rome,
Italy,
Was calling
For her.
A wedding,
Love,
Her heart
Open
For what was
To come.
A meeting
Unexpected
And then again,
Expected.
The script would once

Lotte Søs Farran-Lee

Again
Show its
Magic.

The craft rose from the Danish ground and took the three of them into the air, crossing the countries from above. They watched the houses turn small, crossed the ocean and the Alps, and slowly drew closer to the destination.

She knew the coastline so well when getting closer and grew quietly excited when the plane had to loop, and Cristoforo Colombo, the long road from the sea toward the center of Rome, came into sight. She loved that road toward the city center, with all the trees on both sides. For her it captured something deep within, something was hard to explain. It was just love.

"Oh man, I still love this. My body is so happy."

Sebastian started laughing. "You Roman woman. I knew it."

"It's so fantastic when the wheels touch the ground. That just never grows old with me."

"It's wonderful, Katrin. I'm really looking forward to this."

"Me too, Stine."

"Life is just so magical."

They left the plane. Got their car and installed themselves in the Hotel. The day was brand new and all the streets of Rome lay in front them only to be touched by their feet.

Wine
Foodsteps
Italian food
Cappuccinos
The beautiful mess
The sun
Italian words
Spectacular buildings
Roman kisses
More food
More wine
Two days

Like tourists
A car
A sexy one
Broke the spell
Of Rome
Took them north
To Pitigliano
A wedding
Was to be
Manifested.

"Wow it's amazing." Stine was fully amazed by the beauty.

They came from the south road and were to pass the bridge going up the hill to the center of Pitigliano. The sight of the city from this site was spectacular.

"Yes, I know. It's almost like you just can't understand how it happened. Do you know that Angelo came from this town?

"Do you mean the angel guy from all your trips?" Sebastian replied.

"Yes, exactly. It's quite weird how life comes back in circles."

Sebastian gave her a cheeky smile. "And no news about the mysterious Michael?" She had told him about the "meeting" with the old man, the information she had received about Michael, and how Rikke had helped her realize that it was the old Michael who had been shown to her—the both mysterious and special guy.

"No, no, dear Sebastian. No news, but he will show when the timing is right I'm sure. And with all the work that I have done on myself, I'm sure it is spot on when we meet again."

"How can you be so sure?" Stine asked in a gently judgmental voice, letting her tone reveal that she had a hard time believing you could see something that hadn't happened yet.

"I don't know, and then again I do know. I have seen it so many times in my life, that things happen when a certain energy has been shown to me."

"It sounds really wild, when I haven't experienced it myself."

"Yes, I know, I think it's weird too. But that's just the way it is."

Stine glanced through the window, and Katrin gave Sebastian a "shut up now" look. Even if she was good friends with Stine there were certain things that she preferred to share only with Sebastian. He gave her and *I know and I will shut up* smile back.

They parked the car just outside the wine shop under the big arch. They were tired and hungry. Even if it was only a couple of hours' drive, they'd had a little more than two intense days in Rome, so they just wanted some food and rest before they met everybody in the church tomorrow. They were going to stay until Monday and fly home from Rome that evening.

"Do you want to go and get a slice of pizza?" Sebastian was stretching, already heading toward the pizzeria a bit farther up the road.

Stine smiled at Katrin. "I think we don't have a choice, my love. You're already there."

"Yes, you're right. You can follow or you can stay."

Sebastian waited for them to catch up, swung his arm around Stine, and kissed her. Katrin enjoyed seeing the love between them too. They just belonged together, and it made her so happy at heart to see their love in action.

Six slices
Of pizza,
Three cokes,
An evening
That only God
Could create.
No wind,
Autumn warmth
Touching their skin.
The
Stunning view
Of
Pitigliano
Taken in
By their
Senses.
Love

Was in the air.
And a
Magic
Moment
Was soon
To
Come ….

Sunbeams found their way through the shutters to land on her face. She stretched and felt the thin sheet curving around her naked body. The warmth of the sun touching her breast swelled and opened her nipple. She pressed a pillow between her legs and felt a rush of energy moving around in her body.

It was time for a wedding.

After showering she put on her dress and applied soft, warm makeup. She took a look at herself and felt quite pleased with the reflection in the mirror.

She went downstairs to the lobby and met with Sebastian and Stine. It seemed there were many other guests at the hotel who were attending the wedding, but none they knew.

They could walk to the church, and the ambience of the Italians also arriving there was amazing. They were greeting as though they belonged here. Katrin's love for Italy was still fully on, and she absorbed every detail to put into her inner Italian chamber for further usage. She felt happy and blessed just being here.

They stood a bit apart; she didn't know that many people. It was actually incredible that Kristian had invited her, they were not that close. In fact, it was mainly through Sebastian and the Interrail that they were still in touch.

"Ciao, bella. Who do you know?"

"I know Kristian."

"How wonderful. Let me show you were you can sit."

A very kind Italian man, whom she didn't know, guided her inside the church. She glanced to the altar where she could see Kristian standing nervously. She stood for a while staring toward him in hopes that he would

Lotte Søs Farran-Lee

notice her. Soon he did and gave her a big smile; she smiled back, wishing him good luck. His thumb went up.

She stood for a while looking around at all the candles and flowers. She was just about to sit down when her gaze halted on the best man talking to Kristian. She couldn't take her eyes off him and just kept staring. Could it really be?

Yes, it was. She was sure.

His head turned and his eyes stopped at hers.

She smiled at him from her heart and through her eyes.

He saw and returned her smile, blushing vaguely.

Her heart started racing.

It's me.

I know, and it's me too.

It's so good to see you.

It's so good to see you too.

My heart is beating.

Mine too.

Let's talk afterwards.

Yes.

It was as though they spoke; she could hear his thoughts, and he heard hers. It was like that magic night in New York were they had almost finished each other's sentences, each knowing exactly what the other one was going to say. And now, just by looking at each other they knew everything.

They kept eye contact.

Their smiles didn't fade.

Presently he was interrupted, and his eyes left hers. She turned her head and must have looked a bit startled when she saw Sebastian and Stine entering the church, their eyes searching for her. She waved at them.

"Sorry, darling," Sebastian murmured, settling beside her. "I just stopped to talk to some old friends. Sorry you were all alone."

"Don't worry about that," Katrin replied.

"What has happened? You look like you've seen a ghost."

"Who is that guy, Sebastian?"

"What guy?"

"The one standing next to Kristian. —Don't gape! It looks like he's his best man."

"That's Michael."

"Michael?" Katrin's eyes kept staring.

"Oh, *Michael* …. I mean—are you sure, Katrin? Because I have known him for so many years. You can't mean that he's the one?"

"Yes, Sebastian. He's the one I saw at Roma Termini when I was eighteen. He was the magic night meeting when I was twenty-five. And now you are telling me that you have known him all the time?"

"Yes, sweetie." He slipped his arm around her and squeezed hard.

"Shit, Sebastian. Life is truly amazing."

"Both yes and no in this situation," Sebastian replied.

"Why?"

Sebastian looked at her. With a true sadness in his face he looked at her and said, "He is married, Katrin. Not happily married, but married."

Katrin sighed deeply and looked away. How could it be? She had seen him coming. Why would he be taken after all these years of searching?

His eyes had definitely said something else. She knew it from that deep place within. He was the one she had seen coming for so many years, and then she had already met him.

The organ started to play. People rose to watch Giovanna on her way to the altar. Katrin's eyes met Michael's, and he smiled. She smiled back.

He knew.

She knew.

… They had something special.

The ceremony was beautiful, and the energy of love and joy was incredibly high. She was watching for Michael during the ceremony, and to her joy she knew he was doing the same, and the smile was inevitable whenever their eyes met.

"I don't know, but this may be the most beautiful wedding I have ever seen. And if I'm ever going to be married again, I'll be sure to do it in Italy." Katrin was so joyful.

Stine joyfully echoed her excitement. "Yes, we saw the looks they gave each other."

Lotte Søs Farran-Lee

"I know, I know. I just couldn't stop staring."

"Yes, and it seemed that he didn't have a problem with that."

They were smiling and laughing all the way out of the church. So much love was in the air. They were all hugging and congratulating Giovanna and Kristian and then waving goodbye as they left to be photographed at the square.

The feeling of a breakup was in the air, everyone ready to go to the wedding reception.

"Hello there."

She trembled at the sound of his voice. "Hi." The silence was full of a deep recognition within them both as their eyes met.

"So we meet again."

"Yes, we do, Michael. It must be about fifteen years since the last time."

"Yes, I think so."

"How are you?"

"I'm okay. Could be better. But today seems to make everything of that kind go away."

"Yes, it's so wonderful. Where do you know Kristian from? I mean you must be really close since you're his best man?"

"Yes, we met at Copenhagen Business School just after we had been on Interrail."

"You mean that year that we met but didn't really meet at Roma Termini?"

"Yes, exactly!"

"So you must also know that I was travelling with Kristian at that time."

"You're kidding!"

"Nope."

"So we have been so close to each other all the time."

The silence engulfed them again, swallowing the fact they had been so close for so many years. It almost felt like a theater play, with someone cuing them that they were supposed to be on the scene at the same point.

"Do you want to join me in my car?"

"Sure, I'm just going to— No, never mind. They will figure it out."

"You mean your friends?"

"Yes, but you probably know Sebastian, right?"

"Yes, I do, I have seen him with Kristian at times. Is he your good friend, or is it Stine?"

"No, it's Sebastian."

The words
Kept running
As if they had never been apart,
As if they knew every single part of the other,
As if they were one
But they were two.
It was special;
They both knew that.
The rest of the day—like magnets they were drawn toward each other.
Their words didn't stop;
Their smiles were priceless.
Everyone saw it;
They did too,
Only everyone knew that there was another woman,
Marianne.
That day,
That night,
They kept her out of their awareness.
They were awake together.
They started dreaming together
They could be friends
That night.
They ignored the fact
That it wouldn't be easy.
But joy
And open hearts
Were in the air.
When the night had overtaken the wonderful day
Facts were in their faces.
She was divorced now.
He was married.
Three magical meetings:

Rome,
New York.
It was special,
More than you could ever find words for.

"When are you leaving, Katrin?"

"We're leaving Monday. And you?"

"The same. I'm flying home from Rome."

"Me too."

The deep silence returned, and they just sat and stared at each other as though this sight was the only thing that mattered in life. She saw herself in him, and he saw himself in her. She loved just sitting here with him. She didn't care whether they said anything; just the feeling of his presence was enough. It was everything.

Michael broke the silence. "Even though we have met so briefly, I feel I have known you all my life. Do you know what I mean?"

"You know, I know that. —God must have a really bad sense of humor."

"Why?" Michael smiled.

"Well, first time, we just caught a glimpse. Then I was married, and now you are—"

"Yeah, it's crap timing, I suppose. But let's meet when we get back to Denmark."

"I'd like that."

"Do you want to hang out tomorrow? We could go for a ride in my car."

"Sure, that would be fantastic."

They parted, and the dream world took over. She woke up during the night and said out loud, "I could really love him, God," and then went back to sleep, knowing deep within her silence that she already did.

Sunday morning
Arrived.
Two souls
Were to meet.
A story was told
From the woman
To the man

About her inner travel.
An angel
Had taught
Her to love
Unconditionally.
He had finished her sentences;
He knew what she meant.
She had smiled because he knew.
What he didn't know
Was
That she
Already loved him
Unconditionally.
And he loved her.
Only difference was,
She was conscious of it.
He wasn't.
She knew it was in the script:
Their love to be shared
In the physical.
Only time
Would answer the question:
When would they finally melt?

11

Fighting the Script

You can try to fight the script, let the ego rule, not wanting to do and live the job that you are here to give to the world, but your soul will always show you who you really are. If you don't listen, it will always create circumstances and events that will guide you to self-awareness, so you receive the real you. *The more you fight it, the greater the pain as your soul pleads with you to wake up to* you. *It wants you to live you and not a version of you that you think you are.*

You might not agree that it's the life that you want, but you're here to learn about you and express you.

The more you fight the truth, the more you block your inner voice, and the more your soul will have to create in order for you to wake up.

Listen to it. Listen to your inner pain, and it will then transform you if you listen, but if you run, it will have to call out even louder for you to listen.

Michael woke up, his body bathed in sweat. He looked at the clock and saw that it was only four a.m. The dream had been vividly real, and he felt confused here in the dark, where he was. He stretched and yawned. Then he looked at Marianne sleeping and felt even more confused about her presence there beside him. What was going on? *What is it that I don't want to find and hear? That dream must mean something!*

He walked to the living room and made himself a glass of brandy, drew a blanket around him, and sat in his favorite chair. His mind went back to the dream to try to grasp the essence of it. He knew this was no ordinary dream; he was telling himself something. He yawned again, feeling his fragility in the presence of his naked body to the blanket. He closed his eyes to capture the dream again.

He had been in a forest looking for something. It had freaked him out that he couldn't find it, and the worst part was that he didn't know what he was looking for.

A woman had suddenly appeared at the scene in a long green dress, looking old and young at the same time. She had deep green eyes and a smile that only brought love. She looked at him and asked what he was looking for, and he answered with his desperate voice that he didn't know.

She smiled at him and answered him with her mild yet wise voice. "You're looking for you, but you don't know what that is, because you don't want it to be what you already know it is."

In the dream he looked at her, knowing yet not knowing what she had just said. She smiled at him again, and then she told him about the script—his script—that he could try to run from it, but it would always be calling him to fall back into his script. He was annoyed with her, both in the dream and now. Annoyed with her way of telling him that he was not listening to the script, his script. Yet he knew she was right; that annoyed him too.

He took a sip of the brandy and settled slowly. He felt the burning of the brandy running down his throat and beyond, and then entering his bloodstream. He closed his eyes again and laid back to rest against the chair.

His head was spinning, and he heard his inner voice calling at him: *Listen to me, listen to me,* but a part of him just wouldn't. He didn't like what it was telling him—and why was it so bad? He couldn't understand and blamed it on the woman from the dream, yet he knew she was part of him too, calling to him.

I just wish that life could be as I wanted it to be. Why is it that my head and heart want two different things? Why am I fighting it?—and what is it that I'm fighting? I know that I can make a decision and then follow it, but why don't I want to see me? Why don't I want to find me as the dream just told me?

He opened his eyes; he could hear Marianne's footsteps.

"Why are you sitting here in the dark?"

"I had a very intense dream and woke up."

"Oh … You're drinking brandy?"

"Yes."

"At this time of night?"

Michael sighed out loud and looked deep into her eyes. "Yes, I am. Is that wrong?"

"No. No … but—"

"But what? You *do* think it's wrong?"

"No, I just thought it was a bit weird."

"Hm. Well, it's not." Michael was irritated by her intonation and was cutting her off.

"Are you coming to bed soon?"

"I don't know. I need to be in my own space, okay?"

"Yes. Good night, honey."

"Good night."

He knew she wanted to kiss him, but he also knew her well enough to know that she wouldn't when he was in this mood. It frustrated him, her low self-confidence. It was not like Katrin.

He took another sip of the brandy, staring into the nothingness of the living room.

Katrin .... When he had seen her in that church and she had smiled, he had felt a happiness in his heart such as he hadn't felt since they had met in New York. And the synergy they had shared the whole day was amazing, and the fact that he was with Marianne now felt like the worst joke ever. It was to cry and to laugh about at the same time.

Katrin—it was as if she was the life he wanted to live, the one he wanted to stand next to, and then in the middle of this insight, reality came and swept it away. And then this—this dream showed up, telling him that he couldn't find himself and that there was a script that was calling to him, and it was his script, the script about his life.

But he didn't understand. He felt he was living his script, and even if he really wanted Katrin, he couldn't, he just *felt* he couldn't ... he couldn't leave Marianne. They were not happy, but he felt obliged to stay. It was as if they had a deal, they had something they had to sort out ....

Was the script *Katrin*? Was she the one calling for him to wake up? And why wouldn't he listen?

Ever since he had been back from Pitigliano, he had been restless. He didn't want to see that they could be a couple. But he felt that she had opened up something in him, and he knew that Marianne could feel that he had changed since Italy, and he didn't know what to say to her. He was clearly not happy, but then again he hadn't been for a long time.

It was now three months since he had been to the wedding, and he and Katrin had only texted a couple of times. He wanted to become friends, and she did too. He wanted to share it with Marianne, but something kept him from it. He felt if he did, he would unveil himself to her and show her that Katrin was not just another friend—although he could try to persuade himself and Marianne that she was just a friend.

Within him he knew he would not succeed.

He leaned back,
The chair holding him,
Holding his messy brain,
His messy heart,
His messy thoughts
About a script—
His script!
What was free will?
And if he had it,
Was it serving him?
What was the script?
Why should he find himself?
Was that a part of the script too?
And if he found himself,
Would he choose differently?
He fell asleep in the early hours
Of the morning.
In the chair
His subconscious
Guided him back
To the woman.
She spoke to him
About his script,
About him not
Listening
To it.
He only observed that he
Just
Ran
And ran

And ran
From
Himself!

The phone was ringing. Michael was just on his way into a meeting but saw that the call was his mom. It was probably something about Christmas Eve. He hurriedly answered it, assuming he would be able to cut her off quickly. "Hi, Mom."

"Hi—"

In less than a second goose bumps covered his body, a chill ran down his spine, and he knew that this was no happy news.

"What's up, Mom? Something's wrong?" He still tried with all his mental energy to bring in hope to the moment for nothing to be wrong.

But his heart knew
His soul knew
He would be devastated

"It's Granddad …."
"Noooo, Mom …."
"Yes dear. It's soon."
"Where?"
"He is at Rigshospitalet."
"I'll be there."
"When? …"
"Soon."

His mom knew that asking for a specific time from Michael wouldn't be a realistic option.

Normally Michael would have chosen the meeting. It was always business and pleasure before family and Marianne. But when it came to Granddad, things were different.

"David!"

"Yes, I have to cancel. It's Granddad; he is in the hospital. I have to go. I'm sorry."

"It's okay, Michael. I'll take care of it. Go."

"Thanks, my friend."

He looked at Michael with a deep sorrow as Michael rushed out the door. He knew how close Michael and his grandfather were. Granddad was Michael's foundation, and now he was about to lose him. David sighed as he sent an unspoken blessing toward Michael.

Michael ran to the car in despair ....

What's going on in life? First I meet Katrin, then the dream, and now this—just when I had everything under control. Marianne is in place; even though it's not the greatest love, she is there. The business is hectic, and we're on our way to building an international platform. And now Granddad is leaving. It's like something is telling me that things are not right the way I think they are, but I just can't see it—or I won't. Kristian—I need to talk to you, my friend. Oh, Granddad, I knew the day had to come; I just hoped that it never would.

His thoughts were running a horse race in his mind, round and round.

Michael liked to be in control. Even if he believed in a higher will, he didn't like that such a life controlled his life or that the greater life had a script for him, even if within that he could have his free will if he wanted to live by it. He tried to ignore the inner feeling that if he would listen and surrender to the script, his life would be truer and more fulfilling. But he thought of giving in like that as a way of also breaking up with normality, and he desperately needed to feel that he was a part of something, to belong.

He and Granddad had had many conversations on normality in life. Granddad had always known and spoken with him on the freedom and beauty of seeing his abilities and difference from others as assets. He loved Granddad for this and felt he had been seen, but still he had desperately longed not to be like that, even though he knew that he used his abilities in his life. He saw trends like patterns in life, and when they added up, he knew the steps for the pattern to become whole—like a puzzle. He saw life as a puzzle, and it was easy when it had to do with business and creations, but when it came to love, it was difficult, and he was terrified that the only true match he had ever seen was only an illusion or that he was too timid to actually choose it.

"Katrin ...." He murmured her name on his way to Granddad. She had the same special energy for his heart as Granddad did. Why was it so hard to choose it? What was he so scared of?

He felt his laziness
Couldn't be bothered to go through a breakup.
What if it wouldn't be good with Katrin?
Why was he even considering it now?
He had told her ... only friends.
Why was she coming up now?
In his mind
When Granddad was about to...
He couldn't,
Just couldn't
Finish that sentence in his head
That would end
With
Die.

He parked the car and rushed to the information desk to locate Granddad.

He ran while making a quick call to Marianne to let her know what was going on. No, he didn't want her to come.

He didn't want anyone near.

It was Granddad.

Granddad passed twenty hours after Michael walked into the hospital. He had stayed by his bedside all the time, had only briefly left the chair to get some water. He hadn't been talking to anyone, and the whole family knew that they would have to stay away from their bond.

The last breath was taken.
Michael closed his eyes.
Felt the loneliness being uncovered for the first time in his life.
He felt truly alone.
Though he was surrounded by many,
He felt a hole within in him so deep, so dark,
The hole he had been running away from.
He opened his eyes, looked at Granddad,
And the very seldom tears
Ran.

He looked up and saw the sorrow, tears, and affection from his mother's eyes meeting him.

She knew …

She knew his loss was in this moment greater than hers.

They hugged.

He left.

The hope was still in the air from the family that he would choose to stay with them.

He chose his hole;

He chose the darkness.

It was time to face it.

Granddad had given him an assignment by leaving:

The assignment of him.

It was now,

Only where should he go?

It was as if Michael's soul had turned itself inside out, making so much noise that Michael could no longer ignore it. The death of Granddad had made the shift so he had to look truthfully toward himself. He hated the demand on him that he also had to make a shift, a big shift. But he had to find the silence within him to hear what the voice was telling him.

He felt the urge to run but couldn't. He collapsed, his visions failed, and he had to look at reality—the reality of him, not the reality of outer-world demands. He had to fall into him, fall into the script that called him so strongly, more than it had ever done before.

He was looking at his life, trying to observe it from the outside but feeling trapped, as if he was watching on a screen that was too dirty for him to make any sense of what he saw.

He looked at his wife ….

Marianne was sweet, almost too sweet, as she never said stop to him. She was clever enough to know that if she did so, he would just move himself further away from her. But she also knew that she didn't have his heart fully. She knew that something was blocking him from being fully with her, even though he had never told her anything like that. She made excuses to convince herself that it was because of his energy level, his childhood, a lesson he just had to learn, a lesson *she* had to learn, and so on. But somewhere deep inside, she knew she was lying to herself. And she was frightened that he would never really pick her.

Her intuition had never lied, and she hated more than ever knowing that things between them would never ever be as she had hoped. But she hung on to every little step he did to convince them both that their relationship was solid. From the outside it looked right, but they both knew from the beginning that they were struggling against a greater will, a will neither one was willing to obey.

She gave him all the space he needed to such an extent that she forgot herself. She didn't put herself on a high rank in life, and hence he got his way, but their relationship suffered from her lack of self-confidence and self-assertion. He made the big decisions for them in life, and she just said yes every time he showed the direction.

Her life was in his hands.

He was fully aware that he was a shit toward her, keeping her because he was too afraid to let her go even though he couldn't give her what she really wanted.

He could only give that to one woman ….

"I have to go and meet Anders tonight. We are planning to go to India on a meditation trip."

"Who is Anders?"

"He's a guy that I have become friends with, and he is really wise, wise about life."

Marianne sighed deeply. She had heard this countless times before, and it was just amazing how much everyone else, apart from her, had wisdom.

"But what is so different with this Anders, if I may ask? You have just been on a trip with Anja. Why can't we go somewhere together?"

"Well, Anders is just much deeper, and I need this for me."

"I know, but still … I just don't get it, Michael. What are you looking for? What are you searching for? It feels that it's constantly something beyond our reach together. Are you happy here? It's been like this since we first met, and it still is."

"Yes, I know, Marianne. I don't know what it is. I'm constantly trying to settle within, and I feel that we're important, but I'm constantly trying to find peace within too, and I can't do that on my own and need people to help me. Is it so hard to understand?"

"No, it's not, and you know that. But I'm constantly alone, and you know that, too. We don't have anything together, and I miss it."

"I know ...."

The discussion always ended there, and it went back to "normal." Nothing ever changed; they were caught up on a disc that just kept repeating itself, and neither of them knew how to change it. He wouldn't change, not for Marianne. Something in him just wouldn't ... or couldn't?

His bag
Was packed
Again.
Now India.
A new companionship,
New experiences,
New insights
He wanted to face himself.
But he ran
And
Ran.
Not to be stopped.
Only
Small glimpses
Of inner light
Came through.
He saw them;
Changed direction;
Attracted people
Who were
In tune with their voice.
He wanted them to do it,
Wished that he could
By not changing anything.
He ran and ran
Only to not face his fear.

The fear
Of seeing him.
The truth
That terrified him most.

He watched the skies from the airplane. It seemed to reflect this day as almost unreal-looking clouds lay like small dots on a line forming a square as if for a moment there were order in the skies. Order in something that was so unorganized.

He was puzzled.

Anders was sitting next to him in the plane. They had only recently become friends. Anders was a yoga teacher, writer, and former businessman; he and Michael had met at a conference where Anders was one of the quest speaker, talking about the necessity of doing business differently in order to change the frequency in the world.

Michael had felt an urge to talk to him and approached him afterward. They felt a good connection for thoughts to be shared. In fact, Michael believed Anders could receive his spiritual side in the way that Granddad had done.

Now they were on their way to India, with Marianne silently angry at him. He knew she was not happy; perhaps she wasn't angry so much as sad, but in any case, he had done it, had bought the ticket to India with Anders.

They arrived in Goa after a long flight directly from London. The sweat from the curry sun of India blessed their bodies as they walked from the arrivals to the taxi. At their hotel they crashed in their rooms after the long flight. It wasn't just a normal hotel. Anders had been there before when he had taken yoga classes and knew they would be able there to meditate, relax, and get deep within.

Michael knew that Anders could feel his pain, but Anders was wise enough not to bring the subject into their conversation; he let it be Michael's alone.

Michael had had a good talk with Kristian on Skype just after Granddad died, in which he had cried and expelled his pain, the pain that no one ever saw, his despair at feeling lost and also not yet knowing where to start the change. Kristian had listened to him with respect for his sorrow, which he knew felt unbearable. He could hear Michael trying to run away from himself by talking about new projects while still sharing his confusion at feeling lost in his only script.

Michael woke up with the conversation with Kristian on his mind. He'd had a fine, long, deep sleep and felt his body for the first time in a long, long time. He felt how he did everything to avoid feeling it, feeling fully the pain of being him. Mostly he thought about things he didn't want to feel that were too overwhelming.

He went to the bathroom in his little hut and had a long shower, feeling the water cleansing him. He put on a loose white shirt and some loose shorts, stepped into his slippers, and walked to the breakfast area. The resort was built just in front of the beach, and from the eating area you could see and hear the ocean.

He found Anders by one of the tables.

Anders gave him a warm comforting smile. "Morning, Michael. Did you sleep well?"

"Yes, really well, maybe even too well. I feel so much pain in my body."

Anders gave him a knowing smile but said nothing.

"I need a cup of coffee. Where did you get yours?"

"Just wave to the waiter, and he will be all yours."

"Nice."

He waved.
The waiter came.
A cup of coffee.
Silence.
Understanding
Of what
He was to
Do here
Was a part
Of the conversation
At the table.
Meditation.
Relaxing.
Bathing.

Lotte Søs Farran-Lee

Eating.

Cleansing.

Massages.

Guides.

Now he

Had to choose.

The days passed, and Michael felt restless and relaxed at the same time. He wanted to move on, not wanting to fully embrace the place, feeling it would become too overwhelming. He faced some things but ran away from most.

Anders observed his attempt to talk business with him and sensed that Michael simply was not ready to fully commit to himself.

"What are you doing tomorrow, Michael?"

"I thought about going for a swim or taking a bus trip to the city. I'm a bit bored with this now. It's too much. I feel somehow more confused and very inspired at the same time ... or at least I feel relaxed. Maybe I can move on now."

Anders didn't say anything. He knew too well that Michael had only scratched the surface of his real script. He was afraid of seeing the true script, known he then would have to realize that most of his life was based on thoughts of the right life for happiness and not the script that would make him truly happy.

"Why don't you come with me to an old woman today, a spiritual guide? Maybe she can give you some hints."

"You mean like a fortuneteller?"

"No—well, she can see the future too sometimes, but that's not the point. It's more guidance to tell you what to choose for you to face your life."

"Well ... I'm not that keen, but let me try, now that I'm here."

They took a taxi to her place, where they were ushered into a waiting area. Michael felt unsettled by the whole scenario, and Anders went in first.

"Then it's time for you!"

"Thank you!"

Michael raised himself from the chair and went into her room, full of the blended smell of India: incense, curry, and rice.

She observed him. "You don't like this!"

"No, I don't." He felt puzzled by the straight honesty but it didn't seem to ruffle him.

"So why are you here?"

"Well, Anders suggested it, so I came."

"But you don't want to be here, so why do you want to waste your and my time by being here?"

"Well, I—" He felt completely confused by her and then annoyed with her for telling him how he felt. But then these feelings yielded to a state of feeling frankly intrigued by her.

"I didn't think about it like that. I guess my granddad died, who meant the world to me, and I feel lost in my married life. I'm thinking about a special woman I have met a few times in my life. I'm tired of the way I do business. I feel my magic is gone, and I'm lost. But I don't know what to do."

She smiled at him, knowing that he suddenly had let her in without even knowing it.

He smiled back and blushed, knowing that he had just completely disclosed himself. He knew she saw it, and he blushed again.

"You're in pain with *you*. You're in pain because you don't want the life that has been written out for you... You don't want to change anything, yet you still expect things to change. You can't do that. You don't want to see it. You don't want to take the responsibility. You don't want to be present with you."

He sighed and didn't know how to take in this full, intense, honest assessment. It was too much.

She knew. "You will be back, when you're ready. Go home."

He looked at her with his deep frustration. How did she dare?—but he was too afraid to answer her. He just shut off completely when he suddenly saw it.

She's like the woman in my dream telling me about my script. This is freaking weird .... Maybe she's right, but I just can't see what it is that I'm doing wrong. I can't choose Katrin, that's for sure; I have to stay with Marianne, I know. Otherwise I will have broken something that I promised. It doesn't matter if we're happy or not ... or maybe it doesn't. Ahhrghh—I just don't know. I need to get back home now.

He hurried home.
He ran.
He ran from the truth of him.
He couldn't bear it,
The truth.
He escaped back,
Back to Denmark,
Back to his life
Living his shadow
As he was too afraid to live in the sun
Because
How could he choose
To be
Truly
Truthful to himself?
For him to do so
He would
Have to
Make choices that would hurt others…

12

The Priest

Katrin hadn't heard from Michael that much since they had met in Pitigliano. They had only texted perhaps twice, but time had never opened up for a real meeting. She had felt blessed and ecstatic over the meeting at Kristian's wedding and the fact that they had shared a whole day together. When they parted, they were sure they should stay in contact.

The synergy between them had been the same as in New York, and it felt as if he had never been away. She hadn't paid much attention to the fact that he was married; she had simply let herself enjoy every moment with him in Italy, and it seemed they had known each other forever. Sebastian had sent her a mixture of worried and understanding looks through the night. She saw them and smiled back; she knew that he worried about Michael being married, but that day she just wanted to be, to enjoy … fully … and so had he.

She could see that he was caught in an inner pain. When he looked at her, she knew he could see her soul, and his soul wanted to share his life with her. At the same time he faced the fact of his current life situation, and the split in him came through clearly.

She saw his soul; he knew that too, he loved it, and at the same time he was scared of it. When they looked into each other's eyes, everything was laid bare. She was more aware of it than he, but at the same time he was fully aware but didn't allow himself to be.

Back home the reality of him being settled sank into her body, and a confusion that she had never felt before locked her mind and body. She simply could not understand: when he had been shown for her for so long, why couldn't it be? When it looked so simple and so clean, why were circumstances constantly toying with them?

Why was their love not to be manifested?
Or was it just timing?

Why was God
Pulling his cards like this?
First a brief meeting,
Then she was settled,
Then he was.
Anger arose
Toward
God.
Toward
Herself
For her choices
Of knowing that he would come.
He had come!
But not the way she wanted
In that moment.
But could you want it?
Or was it already
Written?
Was she fighting only herself
And not the script?
Would it ever be?

She knew she had to deal with this heartbreak in a different way. She knew the long story of Michael and Katrin held a higher meaning, but she felt lost, felt she couldn't trust her intuition, her knowing, as she had done all her life. It seemed useless now. Clearly she had traveled a long journey into learning how to love unconditionally, but she thought that the man she had seen coming would be ready for her too.

She had spent so many years following her inner voice, surrendering into a greater will, her script—only to feel as though she had failed, to the extent of not trusting her voice. She felt torn apart by the fact that she couldn't trust herself. Suddenly the gift she had been given at birth to see the path that lay ahead of her felt like a trap, as if it had tricked her into a blind alley, and she had no idea where to go.

Sebastian had been right: it would hit her when she was alone again, but she was so happy that she had enjoyed it fully the day they had shared at the wedding.

The devastation led to many conversations with friends who supported her but also hoped that she could let him go.

How could she?
How could she let it go?
If it was in the script, was she in charge to let it go?
She tried
To
Let it go.
She wanted to let it go,
For her own sake.
To move on.
Maybe he had just been seen so she could see how it really could be,
Not fully experience it.
She was confused,
Sad,
Happy,
Grateful—
A mess of feelings.
The question burned in her mind:
Did free will really exist?
And if so …
Did she have anything to say in this situation?

The phone was ringing. She had just arrived home, made herself a light salad for the evening, and sat down in her favorite chair overlooking the water. She had left the house all dark; a single candle reflected that she was home. She looked at her phone and saw to her surprise that it was Michael. She swallowed the last bite and felt her heart beating hard when she pressed the accept button on the phone.

"Hi. It's Katrin." She took a deep, silent breath.

"Michael here. How are you?"

"I'm good, thank you, and you?"

"Good but very busy."

"But you like it busy." She laughed, and so did he.

"How have you been?" he asked. "It was a fantastic wedding, right?"

"Yes, absolutely marvelous."

"I think it was the best wedding I have ever been to."

"Not better than your own wedding?" She bit her tongue; it had just slipped out. Michael was silent.

She quickly changed the subject. "So do you want to go and have a coffee one day?"

"Yes, that would be great. I'm just really busy."

"Well, let me know when you can, and then text me, I'm sure we will be able to make it one day."

"That sounds great. I'll let you know shortly."

"Fantastic, Michael. I will look forward to seeing you again."

"Yes, me too."

Katrin hang up, feeling utterly disappointed; She could feel that he was closing down and didn't want her too near. On the other hand she understood. She had felt the same way, being engaged to Mads, when they had met in New York. But she felt sad about it. She knew she would have to let him go. She just knew that even if he proposed they remain friends, they couldn't. The timing was not right—again.

She went to the bathroom, filled the tub with water and some lavender drops, let a few candles, and let herself sink into the warm water and relaxing smell.

I thought that when I arrived here—where I would meet him in person—then he would be ready for me. He is not, I can hear that, I can hear that somewhere in him he wants to, but not now. He has something that he has to do. But I know ... I just know somewhere deep within me ... this is our script. He is in mine, and I'm in his. We can't deny it. We can choose to say no to it; I can hear him doing that now, and I have done it myself. But I know we're meant to be. We're meant to unite in this life. It's just that bloody timing.

They next met
In a café.
Their special energy was there;
They both knew.
They sat for a long time,

Eyes meeting
With a deep understanding.
No words were needed.
She told him
That she thought they should let it go.
He felt sad about it;
She did too.
But he knew that it was the right thing to do.
Angry that it couldn't be both.
But it couldn't.
He looked at her,
Wanting her to stay
As at the same time he felt like walking away,
Wanting to run,
Wanting to stay.
Was it timing?
Lack of maturity?
Did the script say later?
Or did he not want to listen to what was written?
He knew.
She knew.
But he wouldn't see it.
Not yet …
So he ran,
Letting her go,
Letting himself go.
But was it just an illusion
Of letting something go?
Something that could never be?
Letting go of ….

She left the meeting with an inner peace, knowing that she had done the right thing. She felt she had been true to herself, to him, and to the greater picture. If it was to be, he would come back. She felt peaceful for some time, until the loss of direction overwhelmed her body, and her tears just would not stop. She was overwhelmed by a mixture of surrender, exhaustion, and loss of meaning. Hardest of all was losing trust in her inner compass, because with that broken, what was then left?

An old friend of hers, Maja, called her out of the blue, and she shared it all. They were very different from each other but they accepted that fully, which created a space for them just to be. Maja knew Katrin's magic, as she called it. She knew that when Katrin saw things, they would come true. That was how it had been since they were kids, and Maja was sure that it would happen again.

Her soft tone helped Katrin relax, knowing that she was on the right track in life, only she could not see or feel it just then.

Maja constantly reassured her that he would come when the time was right, that she had done the right thing, and that Katrin probably had something to learn within herself before he could fully arrive.

But what? What more was there to learn now? She had wanted to learn how to love unconditionally and felt she had accomplished that mission when she had loved her Italian Angel. Now it seemed that she was not done yet.

First she blamed it on Michael that he was not ready and couldn't really understand why he was blind to it, but maybe it was herself too. She just couldn't understand how she also might in fact not be ready for him right now.

She had to set him free fully and herself too. In learning to love unconditionally, she had forgotten to love herself unconditionally. It was now time to be and really *be* unconditionally love toward herself and toward Michael, to really set him free for the greater script. In doing so she felt she would be true to the script, but was he? The idea of just loving unconditionally sounded so easy, but the pain within grew bigger and bigger as days passed.

Maja had suggested a priest. Soon she had written an email:

Dear Per:

I was wondering if you might have some time to talk. Life has shown itself from a side that I just don't know how deal with, and I don't know where to go.
Looking forward to hearing from you.

Best wishes,
Katrin

She had written the few lines ten times, added others only to erase them again, and came back repeatedly to the same few lines. She was nervous; this was the first time she had contacted a priest. She had done a lot of therapy over the years, but a priest— She kept her mind and heart open to the greater meaning and readied herself for what could happen.

She arrived at the priest's house and felt more relaxed the second he opened the door.

They were to sit in his living room and she felt quickly ready to share. They had coffee and biscuits.

"So what's on your heart, Katrin?"

"Well … it's really a long story, but I will tell you the essentials. Many years ago I had a vision of how a man and a woman could melt together, and when that happened, I saw that a man would show up. He did, and actually we have met more than once—the first time without talking, and the second time I was engaged to marry, and then this time … well, now he is married.

"We both know that it's special; it's like everything falls into place when we meet. I love it, and I love him. But I feel lost now. I don't want to be alone all my life, but I know he's the one I should share my life with. And I'm so angry with God because I have listened to him, and I think he has a really bad sense of humor. What's worst is that I just don't know if I can trust myself anymore."

"Well, I've heard that some receive epiphanies. I don't myself, but some see Jesus or other visions. So what you've seen is probably right."

"Yes, I used to do that, but now it feels—I don't know. I just feel lost."

"What if you saw all the things you see as items you could put in a filing cabinet? Then you don't have to do anything about it. You can just leave everything there, and it will unfold as time is ready for it. In that way you can relax and let it all be."

Katrin smiled softly. "You make it sound so simple."

"Yes, and then accept that you're single now, and enjoy that. Then it will all come. Trust your sight, and relax about the timing. It's not your responsibility to solve the how and when, but just be true to you and then just be."

"I like it, I like the way you're putting this. So it's not my fault?"

"No, Katrin, it's not your fault. You have a special gift. Trust it, and stay with it. Stay with you. It will all be okay."

"Thank you so much, Per."

She smiled at him, and they sat in silence.

Then he smiled back. "You're always welcome, Katrin."

"I can't believe that I didn't realize that I could come here. It's been a really nice surprise. Thank you again."

"Come to church on Sunday. It's nice."

"That sounds great. I will do that. See you soon."

"Yes you too Katrin."

That Sunday
Two souls
In different churches
Bending their knees in front of the altar,
Both folding their hands,
Asking for guidance,
Asking for a clear message,
Asking for support,
Asking for help
To be
With that love
That they both
Felt at
Heart;
Asking for the greater picture to take care of them,
Supporting them
To carry that love
And help
For it to
Be expelled
In that form
That it was for the
Greater
Love.
They both
Ended it
With an
Amen!

13

Shreya

Michael stayed in the café after Katrin had left, following her with his eyes until her shadow disappeared. He had said "See you!" She had just smiled as she knew and he knew it would happen again, even though right now it didn't seem so. He knew she'd done the right thing for her and probably for both of them, but he felt the crack of his pain, which had opened up since Granddad died, widen just a bit more, and it felt as if he was just gazing down into a huge black chasm of pain.

He sat in the café and felt that he simply *had* to close down. He felt such an intense anxiety if he had to follow her …. If he did, he would have to feel, really feel again—as he had in New York—and he was too scared of it, scared of following his heart.

Granddad … he knew what Granddad would have said!

"Michael, always follow your heart, follow your intuition. You have something special, my boy."

Michael had closed his eyes at the café and felt he could almost sense Granddad sitting next to him. He could smell a warm sweater full of fresh air and a light scent of smoke from the fire; he could feel his calm presence, his strong, slow heartbeat, and his hand, his big comforting hands. Those hands that had always grasped him by the shoulders when he needed it, had gently touched his face when he was sad, were no longer here.

Granddad's physical absence sent a chill through his body. He shook it off; he needed to feel in control.

I don't know how to navigate in this, and I just feel the anxiety paralyzing my body if I have to follow what I deep down know what is best. I have to shut down, I have to keep the promise to myself, to close that deep feeling of— He couldn't even dare to think the word out. *Maybe Marianne and I can change. Maybe we can become that love that I'm feeling for Katrin. Maybe we can, if we work on ourselves.*

He sat in that café, alone and anxious and trying to desperately make a plan that could keep him out of the real feelings that would make him follow his heart, follow his voice, and hence follow what was said to be the script.

The voice within him struggled to get through the crack, to wake him, to shout at him to *listen!* That voice knew that his soul would be without that inner pain if he just listened, but as long as he refused, it could only add and push more pain within his system to get him to *listen.*

He left the café determined to shut down the voice again and suppress it even harder. He felt the sorrow, but the anxiety drifted away if only he could focus on never being in touch with his real feelings. No one was to know, not even himself.

He suddenly rushed up,
Walked to the door,
And left the café behind.
He refused to see back,
Only forward,
To forget,
To run,
Not dealing with the truth,
The truth of him.
He could do it;
He could refuse it.
And with Granddad no longer here,
No one would remind him
About who he really was
And his script.
Or so he thought ….

"What is it, Michael? You're getting worse and worse, I know you keep saying everything is good and you constantly talk about all the projects that you're doing, but you don't even seem really happy about that anymore."

"I know, Marianne, I know."

"I'm really worried about you."

Lotte Søs Farran-Lee

"I'm actually worried too …."

"Ever since Kristian's wedding, you have been so distant. And then since your granddad died, it has gotten worse. What is it, Michael? Talk to me, please. I can't take it anymore. I'm trying to follow you, and I would gladly do it, but it's like you don't even know where you're going. And it seems like we have nothing in common anymore, apart from our children. But you're not with them either."

"I know, Marianne … I know."

She sighed out loud, and the tears started running. She just didn't know how to get through life anymore. They couldn't even talk about it, and that was the hardest part. If only she knew what was going on, but he just kept on being so damn busy, and it wasn't fun busy anymore. It felt as if he was running away, running away from her, the kids, and himself too.

"What do you need, Michael? We can't go on like this."

"I know, Marianne. I know."

"Are you going to say anything besides 'I know, I know'? I can't take it anymore."

"Then leave!"

"You're such an egocentric idiot sometimes. I have been nothing but supportive."

"For fuck's sake, Marianne, I know. I'm lost—so bloody lost, and I hate it. I hate it. I've lost my magic at work; we're shit, and I don't know where to go. So shut up, Marianne. I have no clue."

The silence between them became like a concrete block where even the strongest drill wouldn't have a chance to make a scratch.

Marianne wept silently, hiding her face in her hands. Michael looked at her in anger. He didn't know why he was so mad at her. It wasn't her fault. He really wanted to love her, to make her happy, but something deep within him couldn't; he just couldn't, and he knew it.

His head was so heavy; nothing was moving.

He began again. "I simply don't know, Marianne. I really want it to work between us—"

"But you say it all the time, and then you leave again. Nothing happens, and I can't take it anymore. And you're not well. I can see it."

"I know …."

"Why don't you get some help? You tried that in India, but it sounded like you were running there too."

"I know …."

Michael kept repeating himself. He didn't dare say too much, because he was so confused himself that if he started to talk, he might have to defend himself later. So he became silent.

She asked, "Should I move?"

"No"—leaving *"not now"* silent in his head. That thought surprised him, as if he could hear it for the first time. Somewhere inside he knew that they were not going to last, but he wasn't ready to let go of her yet. He felt like an utter asshole toward her. It felt like lying and like a guy desperately holding on to something that could never be, but only because he was so scared.

Michael sat staring into space, Marianne was crying, and no words were shared. *Katrin* … why was he thinking of her now? They had agreed—or at least she had clearly said she didn't want to be in contact, that it was best for the greater picture.

She always reminded him of who he really was, and it was too much. How could she care about him in such a special way, when he couldn't even care about himself? It scared him that she saw him so clearly, she saw his soul … and if she saw him, how then could she ever love him, when deep down he couldn't love himself?

"Michael, where are you?"

He heard Marianne's voice as if at a distance. It felt as though he had been gone; he had been thinking about Katrin, about the mirror she held up to the truth of him.

He looked at Marianne. Although he didn't want to hurt her, still he kept on hurting her, and he kept on hurting himself.

"Sorry, Marianne, I got lost in my own thoughts."

It was her turn to say. "I know! I love you Michael, but it's like you don't love me. What happened in Pitigliano? I felt I lost you, and it's like we're trying to pretend we're something that we're not."

"Can you give me some time, Marianne? I need some time."

"But why don't you know? If you're true to your heart, you know right away."

She nailed it. She nailed the truth there, and he knew that she knew that he wasn't true in his heart, but she didn't know why. He did. If he had to face it, then he would have to face his own fear of loving himself, being true to himself, and being able to create the "perfect life," whatever that was. A least he had an illusion about it. It was just that it didn't work out as he thought it should be.

"I think you're right, Marianne. I'll get some help. I need to get straight with *me* again. I know we can't continue like this, but there is so much confusion on so many levels."

"So what now?"

"I'll call Anders, and then I will take it from there. I need my own space now for a while."

She sighed. He had said it so many times, and she had trusted him so many times, but each time he just started a new project and let her know that all was good again, when in fact it was not.

He left the house and went somewhere. She was alone with the kids as always, so she called a friend again, complained again. Her friend had no words left; Marianne had said the same thing many times.

It was time
Even if he had
Made a decision
Not to feel
The real feelings,
Blocking his inner voice.
It was as if he hadn't control anymore.
It was as if something greater
In
Him
Was ruling over him.
He didn't succeed
In any places
He tried
To hide,
To run.
But it kept coming back now.
The reality of him

Not facing him
Was ruling over him.
His script was calling for him
More than ever.
And the time
Told him that
He couldn't
Say no anymore.

The BMW took him out on the street, away from Marianne, away from it all.

He called Anders from the car. Anders listened to him; he knew Michael's pain, he knew that Michael was running away from himself, away from his soul. He had seen it the last time they were in India, and he also saw his denial. Michael knew he had to change but didn't surrender to it fully; hence he wouldn't make any shift. Anders had thought that it would only be a matter of time before Michael would start to crack. He was right; it was happening now. He had waited too long and had run too much.

"You're running away from you, Michael, and you know it. The more you run, the greater the pressure has to be before you let go and start to listen. You have to surrender to yourself. You have to let go and let things be—but you run and run."

"I know, Anders, I know so well. But what should I do? I hear you and I don't hear you at the same time."

"Can you go to Goa again? Alone?"

Michael took a deep breath. "I suppose I could …."

"What do you mean with 'suppose'?"

"Well, do you think it would work? I mean I can't feel myself anymore and I don't know if it's right or not, and the last time we were there, I didn't feel anything!"

"Yes, you're right—you didn't feel anything, because you wouldn't! You don't want to listen, Michael, yet you know you're not listening, and that's because you don't want to. You know that if you do, then you will have to admit that you're wrong and have made decisions that are not good for you, and you hate being wrong. It's simple."

Lotte Søs Farran-Lee

Anders said it so straight out that Michael was lost for words. Normally no one ever said anything about him so spot on and honestly … apart from Katrin, but that was a bit different. Finally he managed to say, "Wow."

"Sorry, Michael. Maybe I'm too straightforward with you. I don't know you that well, but it seems like you're driving around in circles. You say you've lost the magic and joy in your work, that you've lost direction. You talk about how much pain you feel, and after your Granddad died, it grew worse. You talk about how much pain you and Marianne are in, and you mentioned a woman called Katrin, and when you talk about her, you sound like you, All the other talk sounds like you are running away from you."

"Ahh, for God's sake, Anders. I need to do something different. Maybe that's why I call you; I know you don't sugarcoat things."

"Well, I have done it for a long time, but you are getting worse, and you need to do something drastically. You only have one life, Michael. Be happy; choose to be happy, not to be right. Choose you, choose your script."

"What do you mean about the script? So many things … or not so many, but the woman in India told me about it, and it freaked me out as I had just dreamt about her."

"Well, go back, Michael. You need to listen to her, *really* listen to her. She is wise."

"I know, that's why I got scared. Do you know about the script too?"

"Well yes and no. But go and listen for yourself! I'm sure you're much more ready now."

"Thank you, Anders. I will go."

"Do that, and take care."

"Thanks, and you too."

Michael hung up. He knew he had to make some decisions, but the first one was to buy a ticket to India.

She understood.
He had to go.
She had hoped he didn't have to.
She was scared—
Scared to lose him.

But in a way she already had.
She knew
He knew
Right now they were just
Extending time.
But she wasn't sure.
Maybe that too …
Was a part of the script?
India was calling.
He flew.
To hear him.
To hear his script ….

He heard his name over the speakers. "Michael Boel, please proceed to gate thirty immediately. Your plane is ready for departure."

He was running like a madman. He was late, as always, but this time a little bit too late. He had just been sitting and working in the airport between flights in London, when he suddenly ran out of time.

They were just about to close the door, when he arrived around the corner of gate 30. "You're very lucky, sir; the pilot just gave you an extra five minutes."

"Thank you, thank you."

He entered the flight, and in that second the door closed behind him. The plane began taxiing while he found his seat.

Soon he would be in Goa again.

He rested a couple of days and followed the meditation schedule at the resort, eating fresh fruits and vegetables.

He sat down in a quiet place at the resort. He had just been to a morning meditation and did not feel like being with the others. Something had shifted under the meditation, as if strings within his brain were connecting in a different way, or receivers were being turned on in different directions. He drank some water and glanced around; then he felt the

Lotte Søs Farran-Lee

heaviness of the rested body. He closed his eyes and suddenly heard the words again:

You can try to fight the script, let the ego rule, not wanting to do and live the job that you are here to give to the world, but your soul will always show you who you really are. If you don't listen, it will always create circumstances and events that will guide you to self-awareness, so you receive you. *The more you fight it, the greater the pain as your soul pleads with you to wake you up to* you. *It wants you to live you and not a version of you that you think you are.*

You might not agree that it's the life that you want, but you're here to learn about you and express you.

The more you fight the truth, the more you block your inner voice, and the more your soul will have to create in order for you to wake up.

Listen to it. Listen to your inner pain, and it will then transform you if you listen, but if you run, it will have to call out even louder for you to listen.

He heard the words clearly again in his head, as if the old woman was sitting just opposite him. The words hit him harder this time, as if he understood them and wasn't scared of them this time. Was it the meditation that made the words feel lighter? Was it the fruit? The swimming? The silence of Goa?

He had started to analyze again.
He tried to stop the thoughts. He had to stop them.
They weren't important.
The importance was in the words from the woman.
He had to go and see her.
He knew now.
He couldn't run from it.
He had hoped he could.
He went to the reception,
Asked if he could.
And of course he could.
In two days.
He would be back.
Back with the old woman.
The one he was scared of
Because of her ruthless honesty.

But she was a mirror,
A mirror of him,
The mirror that told him
How scared he was of his own truth.

He woke up early and felt an unease, an anxiety sneaking into his mind and body. He felt the never-ending restlessness in his body and wanted to get up and walk around as he normally would, but something in him felt far from normal, and he stayed in bed with his anxiety. He could hardly breathe. He had actually become quite aware this week how little he felt his body, how dimly he was aware of how he actually felt about his life… felt about him.

He took a deep breath in bed and stayed close with his anxiety. He took some deep breaths again—and suddenly a wave of sadness swept over his body, and he started to cry. First the tears ran slowly, but he couldn't hold them back anymore. His body let go, and all the feelings he had held back for so long flowed out of his system. He followed his body into the mass of emotions no longer held back, and he sobbed for a long time, until the dawn began to brighten and the sun started to show its face again.

Please, Granddad, help me. Help me. I feel so lost without you. I feel so alone. I don't know what to do. I feel I make the wrong decisions all the time. I can't feel anymore. I miss you. —*Oh, God, why did you have to take him away? I miss you, Granddad. I miss you so much. What do I do?*

His grief over Granddad's departure had finally burst from his system, and he felt the loneliness staring at him, calling for his attention, imploring him not to run away from himself anymore. His pain transfixed him, and for the first time he couldn't run, he couldn't move, his body simply didn't move.

In the end he fell asleep, exhausted from the tears, from feeling the bone-deep pain, the pain of being him in the world, feeling alone and lost, not listening to his voice anymore. He had abandoned it, not trusting its messages anymore—only to face that he felt even more lost when he didn't listen to the voice and that script that was written for him.

He woke up to the sound of someone knocking. "Michael! Michael, are you there? It's late, and you haven't been to morning meditation or breakfast. Are you all right?"

He looked around, confused and disoriented. *Where am I? What day is it? What am I doing here, and why on earth do I feel like a piece of shit?*

He heard the voice again. "Michael, are you there? I'm worried."

"Yes, I'm here. Who are you?"

"It's me—Krystal, your teacher."

He mumbled out loud: "Teacher?" *"Why am I having a teacher? … Ahh, I'm in India, I was crying all night. I'm doing meditation here. Oh shit, I'm supposed to go see that old lady today. Gosh, I am always late.*

He opened the door to see Krystal standing there. This Englishwoman glowed with health. For many years she had led this retreat center with her husband, Brian.

"I'm here, Krystal. I'm okay, but not the best. I overslept."

"Do you want to talk about it?"

"No not really. I'm just releasing stuff—no. I guess that's a good thing." He smiled at her.

"Yes, Michael, that's wonderful to hear."

"Well, I don't know whether I think it's wonderful, but I guess it's good that I'm reacting now."

"Yes, it really is."

"What time are you going to Shreya today?"

"Well, I'm supposed to be there at one p.m. So I guess I'm okay for that."

"Yes, perfect. The car is booked."

She smiled at him, thinking how beautiful it was when clients came and started to drop their shields. She loved to see when people began shining their light again, when they went back to their script. She loved to see it, and Michael was glowing now for the first time since she'd met him. She knew he'd had a huge breakthrough, apparently overnight. She knew she shouldn't ask too many questions; he was okay; everything was okay exactly the way it was. She knew it didn't feel that way to him, but that was okay too.

"Do you want me to bring to a cup of tea and some fruit?"

"Yes, thank you, Krystal. That would be great."

"Let me know if you want to talk after you've seen Shreya, okay?"

"Yes, I will, and thank you."

"Thank you too, Michael—you're doing great work."

He smiled at her, knowing that she saw something more than he had told her. In fact she knew it all, and he was grateful to her for not saying anything more.

Presently he had some tea and some fruit, went for a swim in the ocean, and returned to his room. He felt more relaxed than he had in years. He had surrendered last night, he knew that he had faced himself more truthfully than ever before. He felt pleased with himself and still sad, a bit reluctant to go to Shreya, the old woman, today but also knew that he had to do it.

He felt so fragile when he stood in front of Shreya's house. He hesitated to approach her front door, to confront her—or to confront his mirror. He was scared. He knew, and he knew she already knew that too.

She opened the door and smiled. Her manner was warmer this time, or was it just because he saw it this time?

"I've been waiting for you."

He smiled at her, hardly daring to say anything, feeling overwhelmed by her knowing. "Thank you."

"Come this way." She pointed in silence to the chair he was to sit in.

He sat.
She looked at him.
Smiled.
He felt anxious.
Told her everything.
Then
She spoke.
He listened.

She was so intense and so present in the moment that he felt completely alert in his sense of everything that was in the room: Shreya, her voice, the smells of the room, his body, his feelings.

She spoke slowly, telling him about the script like in his dream.

"Your soul is calling, it wants your attention. It was your devotion,

Lotte Søs Farran-Lee

your love. You have been neglecting it completely. You have shut off its voice for many years, shutting off your heart, and now you soul wants you to listen, to react."

"I know."

"Yes, you know, but you still run. You are in a relationship where you have created beautiful souls in your two children, but you are not present with them, and you don't love your wife. You like the picture of it all, but you don't want to be a part of it. Your soul clearly loves another woman, but you are too scared to move in that direction following it, because you know if you choose her, you can't run anymore. If you choose her, then that is it. She is the one, and when you choose that, you have to fully choose yourself first."

"And I don't do that."

"No, you don't. You can't blame it on Marianne anymore, but you can take responsibility for how you behave, and you are not doing well on that account."

"I know, but I'm so scared of leaving her, because I would be a real shit then."

"But you are already a shit, and even more for keeping her in the loop and yourself for that sake."

Michael paused.

Only to change the subject.

"Then what was it about the script? I have dreamt it twice: of you telling me about it and my friend Anders telling me about it as well."

"What did you hear me telling you in the dream?"

"That there is a script, my script, and the more I fight it, the more pain I will be in. I can fight it with my ego, but I won't be happy, and maybe I don't really like the script, but the more I surrender the more—hmmm— the more I'm living the life I'm here for."

She smiled at him. "So what do you want to ask me about? Is it because you don't want to hear it? That if you really listen to your script, you will find happiness within you that nothing from the outside can affect. That if you truly listen, you may still find pain, sorrow, anger, and sadness, but mostly you will find an inner joy in all the mess that will make your life feel so rich within. How do you think that would be?"

Michael thought for a moment and then replied with resistance. "But isn't it in the script that I haven't listened to what I really want?"

"You're a wise guy, Michael. You will find the answer to that one yourself. I know you can do it."

There was a space of time where Michael let the information sink in, trying to absorb it. It was hard for him to fully embrace it. She could see it in his face: he didn't like to fully let go, but she knew that he knew he had to do it in order for his life to change.

She broke the silence. She starred at him. "What is it you want, Michael? Really want."

Michael was silent for a long time as she studied him.

He looked at her intensely. "I want to live the magic that I know I am, like the magic Granddad always knew I was."

She smiled.

He smiled back.

"Then go and do it, Michael. What are you waiting for?"

He left her house.
The taxi was waiting.
He left
Knowing it was the truth.
She was right.
Shreya.
He was still not
Ready,
Not ready to let go of Marianne,
Even he knew she was right.
He was scared.
Scared of letting go.
Scared of moving on.
In the next second
The phone
Made a text noise.
He saw
Her
Name.

Katrin.
It had been a half year since the café.
And now,
Sitting here
In a taxi,
Completely confused,
He opened the text.
"All is good. Katrin"
That was all.
How could she
Sense?
That it was all
He needed to hear.
Even though
He had no idea
What she meant.
And then again…
His soul did.

14

Tripping in Signs

An old Italian friend had suddenly appeared on Facebook and was in Copenhagen. Katrin hadn't see Antonio since her many travels to Rome and was delighted by the surprise. He and his friends were available the next day, so they met. She took them on a boat trip in the canals of Copenhagen, and they had a light lunch in Nyhavn. It had been almost four years since they had seen each other, and it was wonderful that they just clicked as they had done back then. It felt as though they had never been away from each other.

She loved friendships like this, the ones where you always felt at home together no matter how much time you had been apart.

They had spoken about the script, the one script each of us has, the script that you cannot or at least dare not deny if you have chosen to live consciously. Even if you choose to be unconscious about it—that's in the script too.

"I feel I don't have a free choice anymore. If I listen to my heart, to my script, to my soul, then I know exactly which direction I have to go, and it annoys me. I felt much freer when I believed I could choose whatever I wanted, but I can't anymore."

"Yes I know what you mean, Katrin. When you get so conscious about your inner script, it feels as if there is only one way to live."

"Hmmm, and I don't know why it annoys me so much, because in a way I'm much happier with my life, because I follow my script."

"And it feels like God is keeping you on the right track. Not letting anything disturb you, and if you get sidetracked, he'll surely get you back on track."

"Yes exactly, like he constantly keeps us where we should be."

They were laughing, both picturing the metaphor of someone sitting and keeping an eye on you. But it rang true, that the bigger picture was holding her on track, not letting her get sidetracked anymore. She felt good; she was keeping the contract with her soul now.

At last Antonio said, "See you soon," and she said yes. After that she was sure it was true: they would meet again soon. She suddenly knew that Italy was once more calling for her.

It did not take her long, only one week, to book her flight to Milan. She had decided to go on a road trip mostly in northern Italy; she would rent a car in Milan and then go to Pitigliano to visit a friend. Then she would visit Torino where Antonio lived, ending at Lake Como.

She was not surprised that she had to go to Italy again. A part of her tried constantly to lock Italy down, but she couldn't. Italy was her; it was a place where the string in her completely let go, and she just felt at home. She had no idea why, nor did she know why she had to suddenly go back to Italy. Italy was the seat of her wisdom, so maybe this time Italy had a message for her again. She had stopped arguing, or at least not as much as she used to when she got the messages about what to do in life. And no matter how strange she thought they were she listened and obeyed them.

So here she was
Once again
Tickets
Airports
Flights
Bringing
Her back
To her
Home
To her
Beloved
Italy.
Had no expectations
Just an open heart to see
What it would bring.

Lotte Søs Farran-Lee

She got to the rental car booth at Milan airport, and within fifteen minutes she was annoyed with the guy. They hadn't told her the insurance cost so much to add rather than buying it with the order (or maybe she hadn't seen it). Normally she would be calm and try to solve it gently, but every time she was in Italy she always saw her freely expressive side more than when she was in Denmark. It was as if her inner Italian woman came fully alive. She both loved and hated it. In the end she couldn't stop smiling at herself; it was a bit of fun that she did it the Italian way here in Italy.

She got her car and slowly made headway through the northern Italian countryside, stopping once in a while for tea, pasta, and chocolate. She drove in silence, letting her mind wander in the alleys of the unknown, being silent with the flow of thoughts, not judging it, and keeping an open mind as to why she was here.

The landscape unfolded in front of her, the mountains that felt so big, compared to the flatness of Denmark. The houses, the smell, the ambience of Italy—she still grappled with what it was about Italy that made her feel so at home, but she could never put it into words. Every time she tried, she felt as though nothing could explain her deep sense of belonging.

She reached the small roads leading toward Pitigliano, and the scenery was so spectacular that she stopped at many places, just to feel the silence of the countryside and absorb the beauty of it all.

She passed a valley and stopped. Just outside her window, atop a lightning-blasted tree sat an eagle, quietly staring at her. She was transfixed by the fact that it wasn't moving but simply kept staring at her. She felt it had a message for her, that this trip would be full of wisdom, it would lead her to understand something important. A message would appear for her on this trip.

She arrived late that night in Pitigliano. It wasn't that long since she'd been here for Kristian's wedding. She thought about Michael when she crossed the city limit sign. They had been so happy at that wedding, both knowing that they were special together, but it just wasn't any good. He was married. A tear found its way down her chin. Damn, she missed him. She was trying hard to get him out of her system so she could meet someone else. She knew that no one else could enter her heart as long as he was there.

She sighed,
It had been long.
She had said
Goodbye.
It had been better.
But she missed
Him.
Missed him
Here by her side.
She loved
Him.
Unconditional.
She just had to be,
Be
In
That
Unconditional,
Not knowing
If it ever would be,
And still love.
If she couldn't,
It wouldn't
Be
Unconditional.

"Ciao, bella."
  "Ciao, come stai?"
  "Bene, bene, e tu?"
  "Tutto bene!"
  Katrin and Paola laughed and hugged.
  "So how is your Italian practicing doing?"
  "Ahh, still not good. I took a break, maybe for too long."
  "But you got it in you, honey."
  "Yes, I know, Paola, but I just haven't had the time to get my act together and do it."
  "Do you want some wine?"

"Mmmm, yes, that would be lovely. What a lovely house you have."

"I know; I'll show you around after dinner. For now we will eat and drink."

"Wonderful, and with the fire too. You sure know how to do it, Paola."

Paola laughed.

She lived in a little house just a bit outside Pitigliano, where there were olive trees in the garden, a terrace, and the most fantastic view over the city. It was a special treasure she had in this house, and Katrin felt at home the minute she walked through the door.

The wine dwindled low as they talked. They spoke about everything, and the foundation for their friendship grew deeper. Katrin shared her love for Michael, with the story of the many "coincidental" meetings they'd had over the years and the feeling of something very special. She told Paola that she had left it for him to be in his relationship but felt that, although she'd done the right thing, she still missed it.

Paola knew what she was saying. She understood that deep love she was carrying in her heart, and the night took on an exceptional aura. Katrin felt once again comforted by the Italian energy, as she had every time she came here. Here she encountered small clues; visions appeared for her to understand and trust the greater picture and hence her script. Italy had really taught her to trust her script in a beautiful way through people, houses, travels, food, and wine.

The next day Katrin went to the city of Pitigliano. She entered the church where Kristian and Giovanna had been married, and she pictured Michael next to her. His smile, his smell, his posture—everything about him. When she closed her eyes, it felt as if he was here, just next to her, laughing with her, smiling with his eyes, touching her deep within.

She walked around in the beautiful streets of Pitigliano observing the Italians, the tourists, the everyday life of this special place. She walked back to a restaurant that stood near the church. It had the characteristic red-and-white checked tablecloths covering the tables. The tables were outside the restaurant, sheltered beneath a very old and wise tree. The outer tables offered the most amazing view toward the center of Pitigliano. When Katrin arrived at the restaurant, the owner was singing a passionate Italian song for all the guests. The restaurant was full of tourists, and it couldn't have been a more classic situation, as if she was seeing a scene in a movie.

The owner, an old Italian man from Napoli, simply loved his customers and the food he was serving.

She instantly felt like she was a part of a movie and that any second the director would appear and say, "Cut!" It was truly magical. The owner spoke with all the guests, and while she watched the goings-on, she ate the most wonderful Italian sausage with grilled vegetables and had a cold glass of wine.

"Hi, where are you from?"

A beautiful couple that had been sitting nearby passed her table as they were leaving. They were visibly happy, and Katrin noticed a ring on the woman's finger with a deep blue stone. She had just dreamt about a ring with that deep blue stone. There was something magnetic about the couple, the ring.

"Hi, I'm from Denmark—and you?"

"We're from Australia. We're on our honeymoon, driving around in Tuscany."

"How wonderful. Had you planned to visit Pitigliano?"

"No, we were just driving and found it by coincidence. It's amazing here."

"Well, it was really amazing that you drove by here."

"Yes, we don't have a plan. We went to Rome, but we didn't like it there, so now we're just driving around."

"That sounds like a perfect honeymoon—and then this place, it's like a movie."

"Yes, it is. Is it nice in Denmark? We have never been there."

"Yes it's really nice. You should go there sometime if you come back to Europe."

"That's not a bad idea. Do you come here often?"

"Yeah, you could say that. I love Italy."

"I can understand you. It's so lovely here."

"Well, have a nice trip on your further honeymoon."

"Thank you and great to meet you."

Wow, that's a bit amazing meeting her here. I have just seen a couple get married in the square and now this absolutely beautiful couple on a honeymoon, with this almost surrealistic experience in a restaurant. And Paola and the talk about love … unconditional love. Maybe I'm on a love trip. I'll let it all be open.

She stayed
A couple of days,
Felt completed when she
Left.
The car took her back north.
North to Torino.
She had never been.
Kept it quiet in the car.
Speeding a bit too much.
She felt excited.
Soon she was about
To see her lovely
Friend
Antonio.
The signs kept
Unfolding
On the love
She knew
Was in
Her heart.

She drove toward Torino, to see the city for the first time. She had heard that it would be like the Italian version of Paris. That was right: it was a magnificent town with the mountains as a backdrop, the wide streets, the cafés, and as ever the Italian light and sunshine.

"Ciao, bello."

"Ciao, bella. How great to see you."

"Yes, you too, Antonio. It's so great. In Denmark I heard you say, 'See you soon,' and I just felt, 'Yes, you're right, we will see each other soon.'"

"It's wonderful that you're here. Do you want to get some lunch? We can go to my office and eat some food there while we talk."

"Sounds wonderful. So how has life been?"

"Well, I met this beautiful love. It's truly special. We have met before in our life on different occasions, and now we have met again."

"Wow, that's amazing. I'm in the same situation, except for the fact that he is in a relationship, and it's just not good for us to be friends right now. I don't know what's going to happen, but I love him."

"I know. I feel the same, Katrin. It's just this kind of love where you know that this is it. He is the one."

"Yes. I just don't always feel I have the patience for it, and at the same time I do, because I know this is where I'm going be when the time is right."

"Yes it's the same for me. Patience is not my strong side, but I guess that's the learning process. By the way, do you want a session?"

"Yes, thank you, Antonio, I'm always open for a new and expanding shift."

They shared a wonderful day together. They had talked endlessly about love, life, lessons to be learned, and how to be with it all.

She received a body therapy session from Antonio. During the session, the deep blue stone came to her once again as information, along with a message for her to send to Michael: *All is good.* That was it, nothing else. She felt terrified; she had left the friendship, left the connection, and now she was writing him this.

Fuck!
Why?
I won't.
At the Como lake
Sending him this.
Why?
Why?
The inner argument
Tensed in energy.
She didn't want to.
How come
She always got these
Messages?
She knew she had to do it.
She didn't want to.
She decided not to do it.
She had

Her own
Free will.
Or so she thought ….

She departed the next day, putting the Volvo in gear and heading toward Lake Como. She had never been there, but just felt this strong pull from the place that she had to go. She had seen that she had to send Michael the message, and all the way to the lake she found millions of reasons not to. But somewhere within her she knew she couldn't escape.

In the Volvo thoughts were flashing toward her conscious mind. As she reflected over the trip, she felt as though huge messages had been revealed. It had all been about love. That beautiful love, from the married couple in the street, the conversation with the newlyweds from Australia, the conversations with Paola, then Antonio and his love meeting—not to mention the session with the crystal.

She felt Lake Como was important. She couldn't understand the attraction, apart from the fact that everybody said it was amazing, but something else made her go.

She had driven more than twelve hundred kilometers over the past week, and everything had gone smoothly. The Volvo had taken her from one place to the next, taking no wrong turns, but as she got closer to Como Lake, it felt like going through a rock. Constantly she found herself going the wrong direction, missing several exits and having to go farther. In the end she went into a gas station, getting really fed up by the fact that she was continually going wrong.

A friendly man filled the Volvo's tank, and she went inside to pay. The woman at the till was so talkative in English that Katrin was happily surprised. She asked where Katrin was heading, and she replied that she was on her way to Bellagio and then Varenna. The woman shared her enjoyment of the cities and how wonderful they were and said she had bought a ring there. Katrin's heart warmed at this interchange, and she felt well taken care of. The woman strengthened her belief that she had to go to Bellagio and Varenna—that an important message awaited her there. It was only her own inner fear that stopped her and made her go in the wrong direction all the time.

She thanked the lady, feeling restored by her energy and ready to go.

So, Como, now it's me and you. No more side tracks. I'm ready for you and your message. There must be something that I have been scared to meet, but not anymore. I'm ready to meet it—to meet me.

She arrived in Bellagio and felt the restlessness in her body taking over. She parked the Volvo under a tree and walked slowly toward the shops and restaurants. It was clearly a wealthy town. Diamonds were sparkling in the shops, and delicious food was served from all the very well placed restaurants by the lake. Katrin was breathless; she had stopped several times on her way to Bellagio to capture the landscape with the camera. She felt the intensity from nature growing within her body, and that deep connection to nature seemed to entrance her, making her vividly present to every second that was offered her.

She was looking for the perfect restaurant. She wanted something classy; she wanted to celebrate something within her, a feeling of being near some information that was very important to her. She glanced toward the ferry, where she had just bought her ticket to Varenna; it would later take her and the Volvo to the other side of the lake. A car with a wedding couple was parking just outside the boat area, with the bride posing in front of the old Bentley. Katrin felt a tug in her stomach; again a wedding, love. She was clearly on a love trip, feeling the greater mission of the trip was about her trusting her heart. The love she felt for Michael was to be manifested; she just had to stay true to herself and trust.

She found a luxurious restaurant with a perfect little table near the water. She ordered a mozzarella salad with basil and tomatoes, a cold glass of white wine, and a view to die for. She watched the ferry carrying the bride and the groom toward Varenna … the love, the patience, the trust, the longing, the letting go, all one mix of wisdom for Katrin to absorb. It had been a long journey, and learning to trust in her love for Michael and its manifestation for both of them felt like her last hurdle. Right now she felt assured by the universe that it was happening. It was only about timing and her trusting her own heart.

It was a learning process.

She finished the wine,
The salad.
Took pictures.

Let thoughts be thoughts.
Let her be her.
Felt the tiredness.
Didn't want to leave.
Felt she had to leave.
She had a message to send
To Michael.
Her ego didn't.
Her soul wanted to.
She trusted her
Intuition.
She went to a bench
Underneath a tree.
Wanted to leave,
To escape,
Wanted not to have
To send the message.
She tried to walk;
Her body wouldn't.
She sat.
Felt a deep energy within.
She knew
She had to.
She did it.
She texted it.
All is good!
Her mind said No
Her body said yes.
She pressed send.
She could move.
Life was weird.
Always letting her
Show.
That she had to trust her heart.
On the other end,
In Goa,

Michael received the message.
All is good!
She was right—
Or something was right.
The bond of them
Was only to get stronger
In manifestation.

She left the tree after she had sent the text. In a second she regretted it, but at the same time she knew she had to do it; her body wouldn't have let her get away with not doing it. She felt blessed that her body was so wise, and her soul too, but still she was angry with the feeling that she didn't have free choice. Something within her was always taking over; she always had to live her script, but she felt that others had the freedom to abandon their script.

Maybe it was just an illusion.

She rode the ferry to Varenna, watching Bellagio getting smaller and smaller. She felt the wind in her hair and the tiredness when she was in a space of constant revelations of wisdom.

When she arrived in Varenna, she felt the urge just to pass the city and go back to her hotel in Milano, but when she passed the sign that indicated she was no longer in Varenna, a voice within her kept telling her that she had to go back.

She turned the car and parked it. Went for a walk and got a feeling of many movies being filmed at the very special places. She imagined the cameras, the actors, the love scenes taking place. She walked farther along to the many cafés and restaurants by the water. She got herself a hot chocolate and looked at all the pictures she had taken. It was really an amazing place.

Maybe there wasn't anything specific to see anyway.

She felt puzzled about why she had stopped but then decided to duck into a church on her way back to the car. She walked through one of the side doors to San Giorgio and went in to light a candle for her and Michael. She felt she wanted to bring out the love for him in a spiritual gratitude.

She sat on a bench and observed the beauty of the church.

What is this? There are so many candles at the altar, and they're all lit.

Why is that? It's just a regular Tuesday ... and the folder here, what does it say? I'll just take a quick look at it. —A wedding? Now? What is happening?

Katrin looked up, and at the aisle near the altar she saw two chairs, two wedding chairs, and a long carpet laid out from the main door to the altar.

She was sitting in a church.
A church
Ready for a wedding.
She had just lit a candle
For her and Michael.
She felt a joy,
A completion.
It was written in the script.
She couldn't escape.
She couldn't work against it.
It was hidden.
It was written.
She and Michael.
It would be.
It was just to let go and let God.
She had come to the end,
Arrived at her
Destination.
The destination she had come here for.
But had no idea.
It was sealed.
It was written.
The love would be manifested.
Now it was just
The when
And the how.
But that she had no control over ...
And he ...
He knew too ...
But was still running.

15

A Restaurant

It had been a long day at work, but a good one. Along with Lars and David, he had closed a fantastic deal with a great customer, and they were celebrating. He had phoned home to say that again he would be late; the silence of an unapproved approval echoed in his ear after Marianne hung up.

It had been a month since he had arrived home from Goa, and he had felt much better with himself. He was not ready to fully embrace it all and take responsibility for releasing his pain. He still hoped that he could avoid the breakup; he didn't know why, but he just didn't feel ready yet. On the other hand he had found his passion for his work again.

Marianne had been happy and hopeful when he arrived home. She and the kids had picked him up in the airport, and even with the message from Shreya in his mind about Marianne, he kissed her and smiled, hoping that this part he wouldn't have to change.

They had made love that night for the first time in a long time, and he had felt quite hopeful that the whole shift was over. Still, only a week later, they were back in the old pattern. But neither of them broke the silence, as they both knew somewhere what it would mean if they faced the situation honestly.

He was relieved to feel happy about work again, and tonight they were going out to a really nice restaurant in the heart of Copenhagen.

Katrin took a final look at herself and pressed her lips together to even out the lip balm. She straightened her new dress, examined her body, and felt quite pleased with herself. She felt sexy and beautiful.

She was on her way to a dinner party in Copenhagen with ten other amazing people. They had all been working on a project together, and it had ended with a huge success for the customer. Katrin felt proud to have been a part of this team, and she couldn't wait to go out with them. It included a couple of really nice guys, and even though she knew that her heart was with Michael, she enjoyed receiving the energy from other men—especially when they were attractive and clever.

> She ran lightly
> Down the stairs
> Entered the taxi
> Leaned back
> Felt a new excitement
> Like a new coming.
> Something
> Was to enter
> Soon
> She knew.

"So, Michael. We've never heard about your Goa trip. How did it go? You seem so much happier now, especially at work—which we're really pleased about."

"Thank you, David; so am I. I'm sorry I have been such a mess lately. I hated it when I didn't feel that anything was going my way at work. I knew I was letting you guys down."

David smiled. "We know, but we also know you're worth waiting for."

"Thanks again. Well, the trip went really well. I felt I turned back to my script—or maybe I've been following it all the time, but I just couldn't see it and made decisions with dirty glasses that made the script hard to read. I don't know, I haven't really understood that part. So it feels as if I'm back ... mostly."

Lars smiled at him. "What do you mean by the script, Michael, and why only mostly?"

"The script—that's probably too complicated to explain, as I'm still in the process of making it clear to myself. But the mostly is because—"

Michael almost couldn't get the words out. It felt almost embarrassing to talk about it, but Lars and David knew the whole story.

Lotte Søs Farran-Lee

"You see, I went to see the wise woman again, and she spoke about some kind of script. We all have one, and the more we listen to that script, the less pain we have in life. It doesn't mean we don't have pain, but we accept it with much greater ease and don't fight it because we're in the script."

"Okay so far," Lars responded, a bit impatient. "And then what?"

"Well—you remember Katrin?"

David and Lars gave each other a big cheeky smile. "Sure we do. You know that."

Lars took a sip of his wine and gave Michael an intense look.

"The woman said … I can't remember her exact words, but the essence was that Katrin is my script, and the longer I deny it and stay with Marianne, the more I'm lying to myself. I know she's right, but I just can't … or I won't. In the end, it's just Katrin: she is everything."

"We know, Michael. We've seen you together, and it's clear that you're running away, which is not hard to understand."

"But it seems it is for me!"

"Yes, I get it," Lars pressed on. "You have kids with Marianne, but are you happy with her? Is she happy with you? Are you giving each other anything real, or is it just because you have security with her?"

"I don't know."

"Yes, you do. I know you, and you must see that. I also know that you're always trying to fit in, even though we all can see that you don't. But it's okay not to fit in. That's what makes you so great."

Michael looked hard at Lars. His brother had never talked to him this directly before. It hit him as if for the first time he really heard. Lars had struck the point of his pain like a bull's-eye. And it felt good. Lars had nailed it, saying it better than he had ever been able to.

Lars smiled back in answer to Michael's depthless look. "I got you, didn't I?" He held Michael's gaze.

Michael gave him a warm smile of gratitude. "Yes, you did. Thank you, my brother. Thank you. I have no words."

"It's okay. I know, you know… and you know what to do."

"Yes, I do. I just need some time."

"You've had enough time, Michael. It's action now. You tried to be normal, but it doesn't work anymore. Maybe it never did."

"Thanks."

"No problem. Let's drink now."

They got some wine, and Michael withdrew from the guys for a moment to reflect on Lars's words. For the first time in ages, he felt he had landed in himself.

Then he laughed with a huge sense of relief. He felt better than ever. They raised their glasses and said cheers. Michael took a sip and then glanced toward the door as a huge party entered.

His eyes stopped
He couldn't believe it
His hand suspended
With his glass.
Not moving.
Only staring.
His friends.
Did the "what?" thing.
He pointed/
They looked
The same way as the finger.
They were
Gobsmacked.
No words;
Just staring.
She was here.
The woman
Of his script.
Katrin!
A coincidence?
Or was it
The script
That was ready
For a new chapter?

Lotte Søs Farran-Lee

Katrin entered the door to the restaurant feeling free and high on good energy. She was sure that it would be a really good night. They sat at the table, and the wine and the food kept arriving. They laughed a lot, and she felt more at ease than she had done in a long time. She was sitting between two extremely enjoyable men, and they just kept the hilarious moments coming.

At one point she looked up, and there he stood, trying to catch her attention. He smiled at her, his deep warm smile. Her heart sped up, sending a deep heat throughout her body, and she smiled back. There he was, and something had changed within him. She could "see" it, she sensed it.

"Hi." The richness of his voice startled her.

"Hi."

Their eyes were like windows flung wide open to their souls. Their deep connection became easy noticed by others.

She rose from her chair and stepped toward him. They hugged.

"It's been a long time."

"Yes."

"How are you?"

"I'm really good.

"What are you doing here?"

"Well, I'm out to celebrate with a team I've been working with. And you, Michael?"

"Well, basically the same."

"So, it's the synergy again." She smiled, and he smiled back with a deep understanding. It was as if they were on the same page at last but hadn't had the chance to fully explore it yet.

Maybe it was time?
They spoke about
This and that.
He was still with Marianne.
She had hoped he had left by now.
She closed again.
Not yet.
Not yet to be.

Not yet to touch.
Not yet to kiss.
Not yet to fully be.
To fully melt
And explore life
With him.
She had closed;
She knew he knew.
He left and said see you
She knew he was right.
It was just
The damn
Timing!

On Sunday, she woke up and made herself a cup of coffee. It was a stunning day. She sat down in her bathrobe and let the play of her thoughts go on. It had been a month since she and Michael had met at the restaurant, and she had felt a piece of the puzzle settle into place deep within her. She just knew now that he would come. She knew that it was just about timing; even if he still was in his relationship, she was certain it was the two of them.

She felt a peace that she had never experienced before, even without him being with her yet in the physical. The knowing had outgrown the doubt, and every time that happened in life, she knew that things she had seen would manifest. Her inner alchemist knew when that fine line was crossed when visions of energy would become manifested. Only she never really knew the timing.

Her phone rang, and she saw his name on the screen. She took a deep breath before accepting the call.

"Hi."

"Hi, it's Michael."

"Yes I can see that. How are you?"

"I'm okay. —May I come?"

She paused and took one more deep breath, feeling slightly dizzy from the reality behind his words. "Now? Here?"

"Yes … if it's possible."

"Sure, I mean of course you can."

"Great. See you soon."

"Yes."

"Bye."

"Bye-bye."

He hung up. He was coming. He was coming now; the moment she had been awaiting for so long was actually happening now. Her heart was beating faster, but she felt calm at the same time.

She took a shower. She glanced around the apartment; it was okay. Took one more cup of coffee. She was ready. The door beeped, and she buzzed back. In a minute he would be here. Why was he coming? Was he ready now? Did he just want to talk? Were they going to make out? Have sex? Kiss? Be naked?—and then he knocked at the door.

She opened it, and here he was, the man she had been waiting for, all these years. Every time she saw him, she was surprised that no matter what, she just loved him. She couldn't put a finger on what it was, but she did, with her whole soul.

He smiled as he stood there. "Hi."

"Hi—what a surprise."

"I know …. I have just been thinking about you nonstop since we met at the restaurant, and I—"

"Come on in."

He just looked at her. "I just couldn't anymore. I have been to Goa, and a wise woman said that I couldn't run away anymore. And my brother, that night we met again … he said just about the same thing."

"I don't understand, Michael. You're saying a lot all at once."

"I know, I just—may I? …."

And then he kissed her. Kissed her across all the years that they hadn't kissed, and she kissed him back with all her love.

They didn't talk.

Their bodies said it all.

They melted.

They made love.

Orgasms rolled in.

Kisses felt.

Love was expressed
In touch,
In their eyes
When they
Met each other
And just looked,
Looked deep within.
I love you
She said.
I love you
He said.
But nothing was said out loud.
It was only the silence language
Between them.
They knew
That language.
The love had finally been
Manifested
In bodies
Being naked.

He had been there all day, and they had hardly spoken. She didn't dare ask him if he was available or what might happen. She just knew that it was the beginning of something new, and he needed time.

She let him go. They kissed deeply, and he said, "I see you," and she answered *yes*.

16

Separation

He had left her—left Katrin, with no words. He knew somewhere within that it was okay, that she knew that he wasn't fully ready. But he just couldn't tell her… not yet.

He hadn't stopped thinking about her since they had met at the restaurant. He had listened to Lars's words and knew he was right. He had felt so free that day, as if he knew what to do. He had to leave Marianne— and then Katrin had walked into the restaurant, and it all felt so easy, just a choice, and everything would fall into place. But it wasn't that easy when he returned home. He felt that what he had with Marianne was okay; they had the kids, the house, and the rest. It wasn't Katrin, but it was okay.

He returned home from the dinner party and watched Marianne sleeping. How could he leave her? He felt a deep guilt nagging him within if he had to leave her. But he also felt that urge, that scream from his soul that just wanted to leave her and call Katrin.

When Katrin looked at him, she could see him, really see him, and he loved it. It scared him, because he felt so naked, as if she could see all the sides of himself that he didn't like, and how could she love him when he couldn't even love those sides of himself? He knew that she loved him—she didn't say it, but he knew—and it scared him that if he chose her, then it could never be anyone else. Maybe that was what scared him the most. He was used to being able to make decisions, to pick and choose, but if he chose Katrin, then that would be it. Then it could only be her, and if she left him, he would always be alone.

Some weeks passed after the meeting at the restaurant before a tiny thing made everything collapse at home. Marianne blamed him over something trivial in his eyes, and yet he knew that he was the bigger ass.

He stormed from the house, furious, and drove to the seaside to take a walk. He needed air, he needed clarity—he needed *him*. He was consumed with anger and screamed something that was far from his usual manner, to fully express his fury. Relief rushed through his body when all the frustration took form, and the water and wind swept it away from him.

He sat down on the beach, deserted but for him and some birds, and then he started to cry. He cried and cried for all the years that he hadn't. For Granddad, for Marianne, for himself, for the kids, for Katrin, for his pain—the sobs just kept coming, and he felt himself letting go of all the crap he had been holding on to for so long.

Exhausted and tired,
Feeling so empty,
He welcomed a vision
In his new clarity
He could see it.
He could see her,
Katrin.
He had to go.
He had to see her.
He had to feel her.
He had her number.
He phoned her.
He drove there.
They made love,
Love like he had never experienced.
They had melted together.
They had kissed.
They had made love.
He loved her
So deeply,
So fully.
It was not just about a relationship.
It was vastly more.
His soul came to rest.
His soul found its space;

Lotte Søs Farran-Lee

It found peace.
He had left her
Without saying he was still with Marianne.
He wanted to be with her,
With Katrin.
Why?
Why?
Why was it so hard to fully let go—
Let go
Of what no longer served him?

He struggled as he drove home. He had to face Marianne, and he'd just made love to another woman—and not just any woman. She was in fact the woman that he loved. How could he face Marianne? How could he ever tell her? It would devastate her as it had already devastated him.

He had slept with her, and it was amazing. They had melted, and he felt he belonged—belonged somewhere, with someone. He had never felt safe with anyone except Granddad. But this was different, and he felt as if everything had fallen into place.

He loved her.
He loved her so much.
And now he had left her.
He couldn't call her now.
He had to sort it out first.
Himself.
Marianne.
Things had to change ….

17

I See You

She and Michael had made love. It wasn't just sex; it was love, and it was the best she had ever experienced. They had said goodbye, and he had said "I see you," and she had answered yes. She knew it was to manifest, but she also knew that he wasn't fully available yet. She hadn't asked, she didn't want to know. She just wanted to be with him, feel him, feel *them*, feel their deep, special love.

She had gone back to bed and lain naked and relaxed, feeling her body's sensation from the lovemaking, smelling the pillow to absorb his smell and then again feeling desire rolling over her body, pressing the duvet between her legs, her body wanting to make more love with him.

She slept through the night, woke up, and took a long, hot shower. She went to the kitchen in her bathrobe again, just as she had the day before.

God, it feels like ages since he was here, but it was just yesterday. I wonder how and what will happen and when. I don't think I should call or write him. God, I love him. Could he just write a little thing? I have to be cool, I have to stay strong. I have to be with my love. God, it's hard.

I'll call Rikke. I hope she is available.

"Hi, Rikke."

"Hi, darling, How are you? It's been ages. I miss you."

"I miss you too …."

"So Katrin, what's happening?"

"Well, do you have some time for a coffee? I'm a bit restless. Michael was here yesterday. All day, and we made love—"

"What? Are you serious?"

"Yes, I am."

"That's amazing. Get your butt over here. I need to hear all the details now."

"All right. I'll be there in half an hour."

"See you, darling."

"Ciao."

Katrin quickly dressed and left. Her body just needed to talk to Rikke.

Her bike took her there, and it felt good to move her body. Her face was one big smile, she couldn't help it, and everywhere she looked, people smiled back at her. She felt happy, from a place within so deep, so infinite. She felt that she and Michael had always belonged to each other, and now it felt closer than ever.

"Helloooo, my darling!"

Katrin could hear Rikke's voice as she entered the front door. Rikke didn't care about the fact that she lived on the third floor, and all the neighbors had the pleasure of hearing her scream. Rikke hugged her tight and smiled brightly when Katrin arrived at the third floor.

It was so good to be here. "Hi, my love."

"So you had sex."

"No, it was pure love making."

"Come on in. I must say, you are amazing. You just know when things are going to happen. You are incredible, baby. You have known it for—how long is it now?"

"I don't know, but many years. More than twenty years since we met the first time."

"Coffee?"

"Yes, thank you."

"I was, like, completely in shock when you phoned and said you had made love with Michael. I have just been walking around. What the fuck! Was it good? And are you over the top with joy? Of course you are; you look like someone who's won the lottery." Rikke laughed her big, loud, wonderful laugh.

"Yes, it was out of this world. He just called me out of the blue. You know we met at the restaurant some time ago, but then I didn't hear anything, and I don't want to push it. I mean, I was the one leaving the friendship, and I just don't want to start something that I don't want to be in. I want him, you know."

"Uh, darling, I know. More than anything, actually."

"Then suddenly his name pops up on my phone, and he asks if he can come over."

"So you said no, of course." Rikke laughed again. She could always turn things into a joke.

"Of course I did. No, I said yes. So he came, and we started kissing straight away. We talked, but it was like a language where the unspoken was just as meaningful as the spoken. We made love, slept a bit, ate a bit, made some more love, and—we were just *there* with each other. I have never experienced anything like that in my life. We melted, melted into each other. Felt everything so intensely. So loving, so wonderful. I love him—"

"I know you do baby!"

"Yes, and I just … I know …." Katrin was gazing out the window, daydreaming and talking at the same time. "I don't think I will ever love anyone like this. He is the one."

"Hmmm, I know, Katrin. You have said it for many years."

"But I'm just so— In a way I wish that I could just find someone who's available, but at the same time… and especially after yesterday, I know I have to wait for him."

"Are you okay with that?"

"Yes I am, but I need to let it go with the when and how. That is what's blocking me all the time, and I don't want it to be like that anymore. I'm still fighting it. I don't have the patience—"

"But you do, Katrin. You're so patient. Look how far you have come. I must say I couldn't do it. You have done something amazing. It's the most beautiful love story I have ever heard, and it's just right here. Right here in front of you and me."

"I know. I just want it to happen *now*, and I feel I give up something every time I don't trust it."

"But isn't that okay? You're so hard on yourself."

"I know I am, but I don't feel I'm quite there yet. I don't feel I have fully given in to the greater picture … to my script."

"If anyone knows about listing to one's script, it's you, honey. You're so cool."

"Thank you, Rikke, you're amazing."

"Come here and get a hug and thank you for sharing your weird but most wonderful love story. You are an inspiration to us all. Do you know that?"

Rikke's arms felt so strong and wonderful when holding her. She felt she could do anything in the world when she stood here. It would be good… it was all good. Just the damn timing.

Katrin knew she had a thing with time. She knew events would happen but rarely knew when, and it often made her restless of being in the now. Now that she knew certain things were meant to be and could not be erased from the script, she couldn't understand why they had to take such a long time. She practiced every day, letting go of the how and when questions about the events she knew would come. Her big issues involved learning to trust—trust her visions, trust herself fully. Life felt like an ongoing test, a test in trust.

She was giving it time, the time when Michael was not ready yet to fully commit. She knew it; he hadn't said it straight out that day, but she just knew, and she also knew that he couldn't and he shouldn't be forced. Forcing was not love—and she loved him. Some friends said she shouldn't wait for him, that she should live her life and forget him. But she knew it was in her script to be with him. She had seen it, and she knew he would come.

But still in some way they were right. She shouldn't sit and wait; she should *live*, create her life the way she fully wanted to. The letting go was hard, but she knew she had to do it.

She had felt so great when leaving Rikke yesterday, felt she could do it, she could wait and it wouldn't be a problem. But already, the next day, she had the urge to call him, to ask him how he was and whether they could see each other again soon and so on. It was so damn hard. She wanted to be with him, create with him, sleep with him, eat with him, talk with him, and love him every day in the physical, not just in her heart. She was mad at God. Why was the timing always so messed up? Why did she have to wait?

She called Rikke and complained. "It's hard. I thought it was easy, but it's even harder know that we have had made love. I miss him like—so much!"

"Come on, baby. It's been two days."

"I know. But it seems like yesterday and ten years ago at the same time, and every time I think I've nailed it, that I'm no longer restless, no longer impatient, I still am, and it annoys me too, because then I know I have

Lotte Søs Farran-Lee

more work to do on myself, and I just want to be done—done so fully that he will be here all the time."

"Relax, Katrin, don't be so hard on yourself. It's fully understandable, and you're doing amazingly well. Relax, find that inner trust."

"Yes, it sounds so easy every time I talk to you."

"Why don't you go to some kind of psychic? Maybe they can give you some clearance or some guidance."

"Are you suggesting that, Rikke?" Katrin was laughing. Rikke had always told her how little she believed in all that alternative stuff. But apparently Katrin had to go through all this weird stuff, and she knew it was important for Katrin and supported her for that.

"Yes, I am. You know I don't believe in any of it, but I also know you do, and sometimes I can really see that it has helped you. And by the way, I heard of some kind of modern witch who's supposed to be really good. Maybe you should try her."

"Uh, that sounds great. Where did you hear of her?"

"Well, some at work have tried her and say she's really good. She treats businessmen too and should be a no-bullshit kind of woman."

"I could use that."

"Yes, I think you could. You need to be cool now."

"I know. I can't take it anymore. I need either to let go of him completely or to really be true and calm about my choice—that I have chosen him."

"Yes, babe, you do. But I have to hang up. Let me know how it goes. And by the way, are you still going to Rome tomorrow?"

"Yes, I am. I need to get out and about."

"It will be so good for you."

"Yes, I'm sure. Thank you again, Rikke."

"Thank you too, for being the most passionate person I know and being so damn true to yourself. More people should do that."

"Thank you. I love you."

"I love you too."

The line went dead.

A modern witch.
Strong voice.
Strong energy.

She would soon met her.
Meet the truth.
Was she to stay or to go?
Was she on the right track in her script?
Was it her
Or was it him
Who was lost in the wrong script?
Soon
Very soon
The modern witch
Would tell
Her.
But first,
A longtime lover.
Rome.

She was meeting her Italian friend Caterina in Rome, and she was really looking forward to that. They hadn't seen each other for a long time, not since the time when Rome had been on the monthly schedule.

Caterina's grandmother, Maria, had died since her days in Rome, and even though Katrin and she had been close at some point, it had all ended abruptly one day when Katrin hadn't understood something. It had hurt Katrin a lot; she really cared about Maria, but Maria had just closed the door to their relationship without Katrin ever understanding the problem. That had been so hard on Katrin's heart that she wasn't interested in repairing the relationship.

She saw Caterina when she entered the Cavour metro station. There was a nice little café on the corner with a wonderful Italian buffet. It was a hot day, and as always, Katrin enjoyed the burning Roman sun on her skin. She felt sad today. She missed Michael a lot; he hadn't called since they had made love, and she was too scared to contact him, to interrupt something. It felt stupid, but at the same time she knew it was the right thing to do for now. Timing was everything.

"Ciao, bella."

"Ciao, come stai?"

Lotte Søs Farran-Lee

"Bene, bene."

"It's so good to see you, Caterina."

"Yes, and you too, Katrin."

"I was really sad to hear about Maria. Was it hard?"

"No, it was really beautiful; she was ready to go. I was really sad to hear that she had just cut you off. I don't know why she did it, but you were not the only one. I know she really loved you, and as wise as she was about other people's hearts, her own suffered. She had a really hard time to show anyone when she loved them for a long time. What happened with you two?"

"I don't really know. I was there to drink tea one day, and we had a really good time. Then I said how much I cared about her and that I felt she was my Italian grandmother, and her face completely froze. I don't know what I did, but she kept repeating that a lot of people did that but it wasn't real. She completely shut me out. Then I could just feel that it was time to leave, and when I left, she stood holding the door open and staring at me, without hugs and kisses. It was so hard. I got really sad that I'd lost her."

"Oh my, so sorry to hear that. I know she really cared about you, and it seemed to me that after that, she sort of gave up."

"Yeah, she tried to call me, but I just couldn't answer. I thought she was too hard on me, and I didn't want to be treated like that anymore. I don't think she was fair. Maybe it was my fault—maybe there's an Italian code that I didn't get—but still, it hurt so badly that I just let go of her, and I'm sorry to hear how it affected her."

"Yes, I know, but it's not your fault; it was her. She was like that her whole life. Opened her heart, and then suddenly shut down, but she was spot on when it was everyone else's hearts." Caterina smiled to herself. "Stubborn old lady."

"Well, it helps a little when you say that."

"Yeah, I can understand that, and I can understand that it has been hard, because she had a way about her that people just loved her straight away for all her wisdom."

"Yes, you're right. It's really nice to talk to you about it. So how have you been doing, any news in love?"

"Well, I was just about to ask you the same question."

"Yeah, but I came first."

Caterina smiled.
Took a sip of her coffee.
They shared love stories,
Katrin about Michael.
She talked about her
Lack of patience,
The pain of being scared to fully trust,
Trust her senses,
Trust her knowing
That it was him to come.
Caterina's love story was different;
She was a mistress
But a happy one.
They laughed about the so different stories.
They ate.
They talked.
They went for a walk
From the neighborhood of Cavour
To the deep center of Rome.
They passed a church,
Parrocchia Santi XII Apostoli.
A message was to arrive ....

"Do you want to go and light a candle for Grandmom?"

"Yes, I would love to. I have never been to this church before, and I have been to many in Rome."

"Yes, it's unbelievable how many there are. This is really big."

They went inside, and as ever, Katrin was left breathless by the Catholic churches. They had something that felt so familiar within her. She felt a deep sense of belonging, as if she and God had a strong history here together.

She took a walk in the big church. There were different altars in the church, and she walked slowly around to absorb it all. At one altar, in the right-hand transept, a mass was going on. She sat down on a bench and started listening to the priest. She started to observe him and felt like a message from the greater realm had arrived. He looked exactly like

Michael—his face, his eyes, his manner, everything apart from the fact that he was a priest in a dress.

Katrin took some time and deeply felt the joy and the sadness that always went hand in hand. The joy of receiving the signs, the signs that kept her trust on track, as if she was being constantly reminded that Michael was the one; she just had to have faith, patience, and trust. She kept on losing those three, she knew, and she kept coming back to them, thanks to the signs. And now here was Michael's energy in a priest in Rome. How could it be any better than that?

The mass ended and the priest walked exactly like Michael. It was amazing. Katrin couldn't stop smiling; he was here, his energy was here. It made her so happy and at the same time, the shadow…. Damn, she missed him. Right here, right now.

They left the church, and outside stood the priest, with a hand in his pocket and a cigarette. It was hilarious; if Michael could ever have been a Catholic priest, he would look just like this.

Caterina was smiling too. In fact, a lot of tourists stood around the priest and got pictures. How often was it that you saw a priest letting go in public?

"It was him."

"Who?"

"Well not exactly him, but the priest looked totally like Michael, he walked like him, his gestures were just like his. I could swear if Michael was a Roman Catholic priest, this would be him."

"But that's so weird."

"Yes, I know, but I keep 'seeing' him in all kinds of men. It's like his energy is turning up in my life so I don't lose faith and trust."

"But you never do that, do you, bella?" Caterina was laughing out loud.

It was so good.
So good to be back in Rome.
Good to be back with
Someone
Who understood her challenges.
And the signs.
The signs

That reminded her
That he was on his way.
It was just
As
Ever.
The
How
And
The when?
Only
Time,
That damn
Time,
Would show ....

She parked her car. She had driven a long way to find the modern witch. She lived way out in the countryside, and Katrin was really excited. As always when she went to a therapist who meant a lot, she was scared of being late, so she always ended up at a sad gas station drinking a boring cup of tea just to kill some time and then still arriving too early. But she just knew that this was an important meeting. She knew that the witch could tell her if she was on the right or wrong track with Michael. She didn't want to spend her life waiting for something that wasn't real.

She had butterflies in her stomach. She had given in to the higher will for it to answer her with the truth.

She arrived. The modern witch was a compact, warm woman standing in the door waiting for her. She went to the toilet as always ... to give herself a bit of time to land. She wanted to make sure she was fully present when entering the session. She was nervous and strong at the same time, prepared to let go fully. Even if she knew she was on the right track, she needed confirmation.

"Come on in."

"Thanks."

"So let me hear."

"Yes .... Well, I'll tell you from the start."

Lotte Søs Farran-Lee

It went fast.
The words tumbled out.
She told everything:
About the angel,
Her Italian angel;
The Kundalini experience
When she had fucked up her soul;
Her pain,
The love she had seen,
The melting,
The meeting with him,
The love,
The lovemaking,
His relationship,
Her visions,
Her longing to truly fall into place.
The words
Kept flowing out of her mouth.
The modern witch
Kept quiet,
Just listening.
Then finally
She was empty.

"Well, you know what you have to do in life. You see it, then you listen to it, then you don't want it, making a fuss about it, and then you do it anyway.

"You're like an Italian woman."

Katrin laughed. "I've heard this before."

"You know what you have to do. You always have to make a drama out of it, but you do it anyway. You just have to listen and do it. Why all the fuss?"

"Well, I don't know."

The witch smiled at her and gave her a look that said *I don't believe in that.*

Katrin saw her and smiled. "That's not true. I do know. It's just I have always just wanted to be like others, and I'm not. I'm trying to make all these ... these supposed *gifts* I have into something cool, but really sometimes I just want to be normal, whatever that is. I also know that I would hate a normal life, whatever that is, but I'm still hoping that I could be that one."

"But you're not."

"I know.

"And then I have seen this man—Michael—so many times in my life, in the physical, in vision, in everything ... and now we have made love, and he is gone again. And I know it's okay. I know he wasn't truly ready, but I know he is on his way. But still I keep doubting myself, and I don't have peace with it. I guess I'm here because I want you to tell me if I'm wasting my time, even though I know I'm not."

"Well, you're not. He is your man. But let him do his thing, and stay focused on your own stuff. You have so much to do."

"Yes, I know. I just want the reassurance all the time."

"Work on yourself, so you don't lose the faith. It's all you have to do— and then write, write, write."

"I know you're right. I wrote one book once. *My Italian Angel.*"

"What was it about?"

"All the things that have happened to me since my Italian angel."

"So you saw it and wrote it down and then published it."

"Yes, exactly as it all happened ... nearly. I just haven't published it yet."

"Well, go ahead. Do that work on you, and you heal him."

"It sounds easy."

"It is easy. You just have to do it."

"Well, I also felt that with *My Italian Angel*, the whole kundalini experience, I needed to learn how to love unconditionally with Luca, and I did."

"Exactly. You do what you're told to do. You're doing it all the time. Now it's just time to be with the unconditional love you feel with Michael. Be with if, feel it. You are it."

Katrin sat for a while absorbing all this. She felt clear when she left. She knew what she had to do. Suddenly it fell into place. She felt the shift.

She felt calm. It would all happen; she just had to stay focused on her own stuff and write.

She had been looking for an answer outside, a proof. Her gift was inside herself already; it was time to fully surrender into her. Take the time, stop the speculations about the how and when.

Her fingers
Started to touch,
Touch the laptop.
They wanted to
Create
Again.
She was to write,
Write the title,
"It is said that there is a script,"
Just as she had seen
Years
Ago.

18

Rome Again

He had often been close to dialing Katrin's number since their time at her place. It had been magic; he'd never thought he would experience it, but he had done it. He loved her with his whole soul; nothing less could describe it. It was everything. When he was with her, something in him just melted, as if all the walls he had set up against others, against the world, could hold no longer.

She knew him so well, every touch, every smile felt like it landed in the right place with him. He didn't know why he'd been so scared of this; he had never felt so good, so happy, so safe with another woman before. She captivated him, she loved him; he was sure. He also knew that she understood why he wasn't calling her right now. Clearly she knew he wasn't fully ready.

It was just this: he didn't know anymore why he couldn't just leave Marianne. It was just a choice, a decision. He was so afraid that he couldn't almost breathe, thinking of it. He was so afraid that he would make the wrong choice. He knew he could never go back, and if it didn't work out with Katrin he would be alone always—and he didn't know why that was so scary. He always took chances in his business, following his intuition, following himself. The voice had come back, and he loved it, but the whispering about Marianne was not getting its full attention, he knew.

He decided to go to Rome to visit Kristian. It had been a long time since they had got together; actually he hadn't seen him since the wedding. Kristian had been back a couple of times, but a meeting just hadn't fit into their schedules. He decided to take Marianne with him. Even though he didn't really want to, he felt he owed it to her. Maybe things would clear out.

The problem was that he hoped for a miracle, one he didn't really believe in—and he knew that for miracles to happen, you had to believe in them.

They arrived in Fiumicino airport late Friday afternoon. Marianne's sister had taken the kids, and it was just the two of them. Marianne had been so happy when he had suggested the two of them go to Rome by themselves. He knew she hoped they could fully reconcile. He wasn't quite sure if it was a good idea to go to Rome together, but you never know. Maybe, maybe that damn miracle would change the feelings in his heart.

Kristian had sent a chauffeur to the airport to pick them up, and Marianne, used to luxury as she was, still felt that it was special. They had champagne and chocolate in the car. Michael loosened his tie to be able to breathe. This wasn't right, and he could sense it for the first time, really sense it down to his bones. He got annoyed with everything about her; every little detail annoyed him more than the last.

He wanted to scream, stop the car, run away—but he didn't. He was well behaved, and for the first time he really understood that he couldn't do this anymore. In a moment when Marianne looked at him and smiled, raising her champagne glass, it all died. He couldn't smile back with that deep love she showed him, and he fully understood that it wasn't reparable.

He looked out the window, hearing Marianne's voice in the background and trying to filter out all his thoughts that were fighting for center stage in his mind.

It's strange that for so long I have tried to convince myself that if I could just feel differently, act differently, we could do that, think differently, do therapy, go on this little break together, and then it would be all good. Then the feeling of wanting to be with Katrin would go away. I have felt that if I could take action, take control, then it would change—felt that it was my fault that I can't stay.

But she said it in India: I have to follow my script, and I have been so busy fighting it, the one that has been written for me. I wanted to be bigger, greater than the higher will. I wanted to do the right thing ... but it isn't right for me.

Michael's stomach felt like a deep hole, when he sat realizing the reality of their lives. He had known it for a long time, but it was only in this moment that he fully realized the truth, the truth about his script, and he couldn't deny it any longer.

He looked at Marianne in the car, and it was as if all his anger was about to transform to his goodbye. She just didn't know yet.

They arrived at the hotel, and he felt so guilty and false toward her, because he had ordered a five-star hotel with spa and every amenity imaginable. She of course would think that they would find themselves back together fully now, and now he felt with the most honesty toward himself he had had in a long time that he couldn't be with her any longer.

Marianne took a shower while he stretched out on the bed. It was a wonderful room; everything was done in such an aesthetic taste that he felt comforted, the way you feel safe when someone holds you tight. He feel asleep, leaving reality behind for a while.

"Michael, you have to wake up. We need to meet with Kristian within a few hours."

"Oh, thanks. How long have I slept?"

"Almost two hours. You have been completely gone. I was starting to get nervous that you wouldn't wake up."

"Wow, I must have been more exhausted than I thought."

"Yeah, I guess so."

"What did you do?"

"Well, I went for a coffee …."

"Are you okay?"

"I don't know, Michael. You seem distant, and I guess I have looked forward to us really being out in Rome, and now you slept for two hours."

"Sorry, I understand. I'll take a shower, then we can go and get an ice-cream. Is that good?"

"Yes, sure."

He hurried to the bathroom and showered. The water warmed his body and relaxed his muscles. He felt the tension of being in this situation, in a loop that the water could only partially release. He was thinking about sex. He felt lust, but not toward Marianne, and she probably assumed it was going to take place … as she was fully entitled to do. They hadn't had sex again for some time; he constantly had excuses—too busy, too tired, too whatever—but the truth was he was not interested in her. He had tried the best sex ever, and would it be like going backward. —Ahh, he was just an asshole.

He got out of the shower and quickly dressed. Marianne smiled when he was ready. Now it was time to experience Rome.

They were going to meet Kristian and Giovanna at a restaurant, Da Felice, at eight p.m., so they did have a couple of hours together before that and in some way it went okay. They went to see some of the art at the Museo di Roma. He was halfway present through the time they spent. He was nervous to see Kristian. He knew that Kristian would see through him, see that something was really wrong.

Marianne seemed not fully aware that he was no longer available for her, or else she was pretending that everything was fine.

"I think we should head off for the restaurant now, Michael."

"Yes, that sounds like a good idea. I'll get a taxi for us."

"They say it's really good Italian food at that restaurant."

"Yes, so I heard."

Marianne was trying to get the conversation going. He knew she hated the silence between them. Normally she had a lot of tasks she could do, but, here in Rome the silence became even more obvious, and she hated it. The silence between them spoke of how far apart they actually were. It wasn't a pleasant silence but painful, because when they both left the noise, it became obvious that they couldn't be together anymore. Beyond that, the silence emphasized that neither of them could address it. What was unsaid said it all.

They arrived at the restaurant, and relief was in the air when they saw that Kristian and Giovanna were already there.

They exchanged ciaos and kisses. "So good to see you, Kristian and Giovanna. You both look so amazing."

"Thank you, my friend. I'm sorry I can't say that about you." Kristian's eyes were so intense, and Michael could only offer him a look that was meant to say, *Not now*. He hoped Kristian would grasp that they would talk it out later.

The wine kept coming. The food was divine, and so were the bottles.

It ended with grappa—a lot of grappa, in fact— and after that they found a bar with more bottles to consume. Marianne and Giovanna at length gave up and took a taxi back. Marianne had hoped that Michael would follow her, but she also knew that Kristian and Michael needed time together, so she had taken the taxi a bit unwillingly.

They were drunk, but today it was helpful, as Michael just opened up as he normally never really did. He needed his friend—not for advice but for letting go. He needed to confess, and the best way was with Kristian.

"So let me know, my friend, why do you both look so miserable?"

Michael took a sip of his wine and drew a deep breath. "I—I slept with Katrin."

"What? Does Marianne know?"

"No, she doesn't, and she doesn't need to."

"Well, she probably senses it anyway."

"I know, and I'm an idiot. I know that. I have gone too long, hoping that it could be good, that we could work it out—hoping I could get Katrin out of my heart, and I don't know. —Well, I do know that it has taken me this long because I didn't wanted to look like a failure, the failure I have always felt that I was."

"But you are not, Michael."

"I know, in a way, but still I guess I haven't ever been truly happy about me. Granddad was always the one who kept that going for me or always reminded me of that side of me that I couldn't see. Then when he died, it became so obvious, so clear how much I don't listen to me, the one I really am, the real feelings, the truth about me. I haven't wanted to out of fear that I'd have to break up with Marianne, and then the picture I had built up against the true me would fall apart."

"Michael, you're deep today. Like really deep."

"Maybe it's because I haven't seen you for so long. Maybe it's Rome—or just the fact that when we arrived, I sat in the car and looked at Marianne, and I just knew I couldn't do it anymore. That it was over, and now I have brought her here, and she probably thought it would all work out, but it has just made the decision even more obvious to us both, even though neither of us has said it."

"Honestly, I'm glad to hear it. Although it's never fun, you haven't been happy for so long, neither of you."

"I know. I'm drunk, and I'm going to leave Marianne; that's for sure."

"Chin-chin, my dear friend, for a fucked-up life."

"Chin-chin, my friend."

They drank in silence. Then Kristian smiled warmly at Michael and gave him a hug. "You'll be fine, my friend. Never work against the one you really are. There is no point in that; life is too short, and in the end we will never be happy if we don't."

"You're right. It's time to choose myself fully."

They drank to honesty
To life
When chosen
From the truth that the script
When heeded
When acted upon
Could truly unfold
Its
Magic.
His head hit the pillow
In a strange form
Of relief.
He knew he should create a breakup.
He knew it was right.
He knew she would be heartbroken.
But he knew
That he would be truthful,
Truthful
To the script.
And that
Was worth
Much more that you could ever
Imagine.

They arrived home late Sunday night. The whole day had been awful; neither of them had said a lot. Sex hadn't happened, and it was like the final closure; Now one of them just had to speak.

He couldn't say it in Rome—that would be too harsh—but he needed to do it soon.

He took a day off Monday, although he didn't tell Marianne.

He had looked at her that morning, knowing it would be the last day.

He knew Marianne could see it, see the inevitable: that he would part from her soon. He could see the grief in her eyes. She didn't say anything … she just knew, knew that she could no longer fight for him, fight for them.

Lotte Søs Farran-Lee

He left home in the morning and went for a walk at the beach. He needed the wind, he needed the earth. He needed to be alone. He got back to his car. He was just about to call Katrin but couldn't; it was too soon. He had to do the breakup.

The kids were sleeping. He had come home quite late but for him it was quite early, and Marianne had felt it.

He went to the kids' room.
Saw them sleeping.
Felt gratitude.
Felt sorrow.
It was time.
He went to the kitchen and looked at her.
She looked back.
She knew.
Her eyes filled with tears.

"You're leaving me, right?"
"Yes, I am."

He tried to hold her.
Tried to take away her pain.
She was screaming as she had never done before.
She couldn't hold herself together.
She hated him.
But she had known,
Known it for a long time;
Wouldn't see it,
Wouldn't feel it,
That it had always been
In the
Script
For them to part.

"Hi, Katrin."

"Hi Michael."

He had finally phoned her, had wanted to for the last month. It had been such a mess at home, and he had to get it all sorted out, but now he felt relieved, as if a heavy burden had been taken off his shoulders. He felt much clearer, much happier, and he hated to see that Marianne didn't seem to feel the same. That made it harder, and it had made it harder to contact Katrin.

He had wanted to so many times but had felt the distress rather than the expansion, so he had left it.

Finally he had taken action. He had phoned her, incredibly nervous as he entered the number.

But when she picked up her phone, and he heard her voice, he melted. "How are you? I'm sorry, or I don't know if I should be sorry, but I just couldn't call you. You see—"

"Yes, I knew you were still in a relationship, right?"

"Yes. You just know me."

He could hear her smile in the phone. "You know I do."

"I'm calling because … I'm getting a divorce now, and—I really wanted to talk to you, but I just couldn't before. It's been a mess."

"I can understand that. I know it. It's hard to go through. So how are you with it all?"

"Well, I feel it's the right thing. It's just never easy with divorces, I guess."

"How long have you known?" Katrin held her breath she didn't want to hear that it had just hit him. She wanted to hear that he wanted her.

"Somewhere in me I have known it for a long time. I just didn't want to listen to the script—my script."

Katrin smiled. He was talking about the script too. He knew. She knew. That synergy between them was special. It was one of a kind, and now he was free.

She hardly dared to say anything; she was hoping beyond hope that he wanted to meet. "The script … yes, I know. You can try, but it just never works out when you don't listen to it."

"I know … I tried …."

There was a beautiful, intense silence.

"I called—I mean, do you want to drink a cup of coffee one day? I just need to sort of get through the worst." He was so nervous that she would say no that he held his breath. He had been afraid that she was angry because he hadn't called her since they'd made love, but she wasn't angry. She was just very, very special. He knew. He loved her from very deep within.

Her response came quickly. "I would love to, Michael. Get things sorted out in a good way. I'm here, and I will look forward to seeing you."

"I'm so happy to hear that. Thank you. Thank you for holding the space."

"You're welcome. Always."

"Yes ... always."

Always
Was with them always.
And now the always
Was about to manifest.
Soon
When he
Was fully ready.
Love
Expressed from a love
That was always
Indeed
Always.

19

Can You Not, Not Listen to the Script?

"Do you believe that you cannot not listen to your script?" Michael asked Katrin.

They had met after his divorce and had taken the time to meet, really meet each other and surrender into their love, and now they were sitting at the restaurant by Lake Como in Bellagio. She had shown him the place where she had sent him a text saying, *All is good*. She was eating the Caprese salad again, and he had sea bass ; the white wine stood fresh on the table.

He smiled at her, that warm, deep smile where he let her see his full soul. He was no longer hiding from himself, and she loved seeing him like this. Life had been fully expanding since they had surrendered into their love. They didn't only become one when melting into their love, they became much more. Now, when they were together, they could shine even more than just as their separate selves.

"Yes, I do believe that we have the free will to stop listening, but I think we hurt ourselves even more when we do that. Why? What's on your mind?"

"Well, I haven't listened for a long time. I didn't want to listen to what my voice really said to me; I wanted to do it right. So you can say I didn't listen to my script and it hurt me, but not listening—isn't that a part of the script too?"

"Yes, I think so. Your pain made you listen … so maybe it's not so much about whether you listen to your script, because the pain made you do it. But I think there are two kinds of pain. When you follow your script, then pain will also be a part of it, but you know that it's okay from a much bigger perspective: it's your soul. But when it feels like you're not following the script, then it's because your ego wants to have the higher will, and that it can never have. That pain I believe is much different."

Michael was really intense now. He wanted to grasp it; he wanted to understand it. Life and people had been crossing his path in a way that he couldn't possibly have made up or arranged.

"I guess I feel that I didn't want to follow the script; I didn't want to listen to what it told me. I thought I would be happier if I decided how things should be … how life should be … but it wasn't until I let it all go and let the script stand for itself that I found peace with what is."

"Beautifully said, Michael."

"Yeah, maybe. The whole journey with meeting myself and you popping up has been really magical. It has shown me that there is something greater laid out for us, and our job is to listen this very moment all the time and then take the action to unfold our script."

They both sat for a while sipping their wine, reflecting. Katrin continued: "I think the assignment we've been given in this life is to listen to the script to fully live our potential. I believe we have different scripts, and we have been given the free will to listen to them."

"Then if we don't listen to it, that's a part of the script too."

"Yes, I believe that in some way it is, but it's very subtle."

"So do you believe that everything is written?"

"Both yes and no."

"What do you mean?"

"I believe that the greater script has been written, and we have free choice about how we want to listen to it, be with it. But then again I also believe that there are parts of our script that we can affect much more than we think we can. The assignment to life is that we have to be so aware so we can distinguish between the two parts. It's not easy, but the stronger we become in our awareness, the better we can see it."

"I like the way you describe it. I guess I have spent time trying to control and create parts that were given, that couldn't be any different. But the timing and the will of everything pulled the puzzle together at the right time.

"Yes, I guess so. It probably couldn't have been any different."

"No, but I'm happy that the pain helped me see that I had to be with you."

Katrin smiled and leaned forward. Michael did the same, and their lips met.

"Are you done eating?"

Lotte Søs Farran-Lee

"Yes, my love."

"Then let's go to Varenna. I want to show you a place that's very special to me. It's where I knew that we two should be together. It was a day that helped me stop doubting but left a deep mark that one day you would come."

"I would love to."

They got the car and drove to the little ferry that would take them to Varenna from Bellagio. With the car stopped, he had his arms around her. She leaned back and felt his deep heart energy when holding her. She absorbed the energy from Lake Como. She loved it here, and this time Michael was with her.

Michael had let go and listened to his script. He felt such happiness—a happiness he had known only when Granddad was with him. He had come home, as though life had fallen in the right order, and as Katrin always said, there was now universal order. It was not a bad way of putting words to it.

The ferry docked at Varenna, and Michael drove the car gently into the little treasure of a town. They parked near the church.

Michael took her hand. "So what's the special part?"

"As I told you, I was on this very special road trip, and when I arrived at this town, I was so tired. I felt the whole trip had told me that it was you, and I must just have patience. My doubt diminished a lot on that trip, and I could breathe. So I was really full when arriving here. I basically just drove through the city, but then I felt I had to come back, and I did."

"So you never really saw the town in the first place."

"No, I just wanted to go home to my hotel, but then I came back, and I passed this church. You know I love churches, so I went in at the side door. Come, let me show you."

They walked through the door into the church, seeing where you lit the candles on the right and all the pews on the left.

"Wow. It's beautiful in here."

"Yes, I know. It's very fresh and very deep at the same time. So then I went to light a candle for you and me, for our love. Because the whole trip had been so full of information I felt it was a beautiful way of letting God know that I had seen it all and that I knew it was you."

"You are so beautiful, Katrin, so special." Michael looked at her, with moist eyes that showed all his love. He was so moved by her love, by her trust, that she had waited for him, had trusted her love. He had no idea how it was when someone just loved you unconditionally, and at this moment at last he understood. He understood that she loved him fully and she had listened to her script, his script, and their script. She had been truthful to her heart and to the script.

He felt blessed, and an inner warmth spread in his body. He felt that he was taken care of in a much greater perspective that he could ever grasp. He had believed, but now he knew. He could see it, he could feel it.

Katrin was moved. She could feel him, and she knew that he knew now the love she had always felt for him and how she had trusted he would come, that it was in the script that he would come, and the only thing she could do while he was out looking for himself was to let him go and love him.

She broke the silence with a fine voice letting him know how she suddenly had seen the candles, many candles glowing at the altar. The church was ready for something.

"Then what?"

"Well, I sat down and let myself be. Then I suddenly saw a piece of paper in front of me on the pew. It was information about the upcoming celebration of a wedding. I was sitting in the middle of a church where a wedding was prepared on a Tuesday. At that point I just knew; if I knew before this second, it was almost a joke, like someone cutting it out in cardboard so I couldn't doubt anymore."

"It's amazing, Katrin, that you can read life like that. That you can read through the lines in life and see it. You know it."

"Yes, I guess so. It's a gift—a gift I used to see as a curse. But it's not."

They looked deep within,
Within themselves,
Within each other.
They both knew it
But they
Didn't say
It.

Somehow they both knew
That there would
Be two
Yeses coming.

They left the church and drove to the hotel. A long journey was behind them, and now it was time to fully embrace the next chapter in their life, always growing more conscious of more light to be manifest for the script to shine the brightest ....

Can you ever really
Not follow the script?
The script
Has been given us
To find
Our way.
Find that way
Where when listened to
We
Shine
The most.
We become
The light.
Only that we
Have always been
And will always be.
So maybe
You can never
Ever follow
Your script.
But you can choose
Wanting to
Shine
Your full
Potential.

20

A Wedding in Varenna

It was summer.
A white dress,
A black suit,
A full church,
Location:
Varenna.
They had come back;
It was their turn.
Soon
Two yeses to God
Would be clear.
She had waited.
He had waited.
Two
Journeys
Had melted
Into one.

It had been in the script
All the way,
But only choices
And time
Could unfold
It,
Unfold
It in the universal order
As
Created.

You could listen;
You could fight.
It was everyone's choice.
Now two souls
Had opened their
Hearts to the true
Blessing
Of their script.
They stood at the altar
Moved,
Happy,
So deeply in love.
They said yes
To themselves,
To their scripts,
To each other,
To love.

21

"So how was your night last night?"

Michael moved on his side and drew her body toward him. She loved it. She loved his smell, his beard, his hairy chest, and the fact that he was naked. She smiled. Just waking up with him gave her a happiness that was overwhelmingly joyful. She let him hold her, felt his naked skin, felt his morning happiness and his touch over her naked skin. He made a deep brum with his eyes closed and just let her crawl further into him. She loved him; he loved her. It was magical that they were now a married couple.

"Last night was good. He was really intense, clever and intense—also a bit too egocentric."

"Just like you," he added.

He laughed, and Katrin tickled him. He grabbed her and tickled her back. She laughed even more. He kissed her, and she kissed back, a long, deep kiss.

"You cheeky bastard."

"But you are intense and really clever."

"Thank you, honey, but I'm not that ego."

"You know, honey, that you're not."

He gave her that deep, warm smile that made her fall even more in love with him every time she looked at him.

Michael always knew exactly what to say, and she felt safe, she felt at home.

"But it was good … in the end it became good. I got a connection with him."

"So you think he can help you?"

"No I don't think he can help me. But I can discuss my thoughts out loud, and I think that will make the book even better. And he said yes."

"You're so brilliant, my darling. It will be your best book ever: *It's Said that There Is a Script.*" Michael tasted the words while saying them out loud. "It's such a good title."

"So it will be better than this one?"

"Yes, or at least just as good. You must remember that in this one, we got each other."

"Yes, and nothing can beat that."

Printed in the United States
By Bookmasters